"A strong collection of tales from all populations of the United States . . . that feature female counterparts of tall-tale heroes. Pinkney's illustrations underscore the strength of the heroines."

—*The Horn Book*

"Even in the realm of folklore, it is the stories of women that most often go untold. With careful research, accuracy, humor, and a wide-ranging cultural sensibility, San Souci's book takes a big step in the direction of rectifying that problem. His retellings are lively and, in many cases, magical."

—Joe Bruchac

"San Souci's language has the rhythm of oral language, and his research ties each story firmly to its region. It's about time we had such a book to share with young readers of either gender."

—Gloria Houston

"San Souci has varied his retellings to suit the style of each story, and his introductions, source notes, and bibliography are commendably thorough. . . . This is a first-class resource."

—*The Bulletin of the Center for Children's Books*

## Other Puffin Books You May Enjoy

# Cut From the Same Cloth

## AMERICAN WOMEN OF MYTH, LEGEND, AND TALL TALE

COLLECTED AND TOLD BY

## ROBERT D. SAN SOUCI

ILLUSTRATED BY **BRIAN PINKNEY**

INTRODUCTION BY JANE YOLEN

PUFFIN BOOKS

PUFFIN BOOKS
Published by the Penguin Group
Penguin Putnam Books for Young Readers, 345 Hudson Street, New York, New York 10014, U.S.A.
Penguin Books Ltd, 27 Wrights Lane, London W8 5TZ, England
Penguin Books Australia Ltd, Ringwood, Victoria, Australia
Penguin Books Canada Ltd, 10 Alcorn Avenue, Toronto, Ontario, Canada M4V 3B2
Penguin Books (N.Z.) Ltd, 182-190 Wairau Road, Auckland 10, New Zealand

Penguin Books Ltd, Registered Offices: Harmondsworth, Middlesex, England

First published in the United States of America by Philomel Books,
a division of The Putnam & Grosset Group, 1993
Published by Puffin Books, a division of Penguin Putnam Books for Young Readers, 2000

1 3 5 7 9 10 8 6 4 2

Text copyright © Robert D. San Souci, 1993
Illustrations copyright © Brian Pinkney, 1993
Introduction copyright © Jane Yolen, 1993. Reprinted by permission of Curtis Brown, Ltd.
All rights reserved

THE LIBRARY OF CONGRESS HAS CATALOGED THE PHILOMEL EDITION AS FOLLOWS:
San Souci, Robert D. Cut from the same cloth:
American women of myth, legend, and tall tale / by Robert D. San Souci ;
illustrated by Brian Pinkney. p. cm.
Includes bibliographical references.
Summary: A collection of twenty stories about legendary American women,
drawing from folktales, popular stories, and ballads.
1. Tales—United States. 2. Tall Tales—United States. 3. Women—United States—Folklore.
[1. Folklore—United States. 2. Tall tales. 3. Women—Folklore.]
I. Pinkney, J. Brian, ill. II. Title.
PZ8.1.S227Si 1993 398.21'082—dc20 92-5233 CIP AC
ISBN 0-399-21987-0

This edition ISBN 0-698-11811-1

Printed in the United States of America

# Contents

CANADA

Bess Call
Drop Star
Star Maiden
Molly Cottontail
Susanna
and Simon
Annie Christmas
Sal Fink
Old Sally Cato
Sweet Betsey
Pohaha
Pale-Faced
Lightning
Sister Fox
Hekeke
Otoonah
Hiiaka

# Preface

SEVERAL YEARS AGO, when I was preparing a collection of stories of some legendary American folk heroes, I searched for accounts of American heroines. But my research into American folklore revealed a lack of female heroes who might be kin to a Paul Bunyan or a Pecos Bill.

It *seemed* as though the American folk heroes of the fictional variety were only *male* figures: gigantic loggers (Paul Bunyan), sailors (Old Stormalong), frontiersmen (Davy Crockett—not the historical man, but the b'ar-wresting, cyclone-taming demigod as rewritten and expanded by storytellers), railroad workers (John Henry), and steelworkers (Joe Magarac).

Eventually, I told the story of Pecos Bill's giant-size "bouncing bride," Slue-Foot Sue, and Lucy (who is sometimes known as Polly Ann), the steel-driving wife of John Henry. And I had already retold the tale of the Eskimo woman who became the goddess known as "The Old Woman of the Sea," in my book *Song of Sedna*.

To be sure, America has more than its fair share of historical women who sparked the popular imagination and around whom grew some fairly tall tales. But robust characters such as Annie Oakley, Calamity Jane, Belle Starr, and so on shouldered their way into popular literature because they *existed*. I was still frustrated by the fact that these heroines remained "human-scale"—not the imaginary, exaggerated figures I sought.

With the enthusiastic assistance of an editor as caught up in the search as I had become, I redoubled my investigation of old books; specialized libraries; the work of scholars in the fields of folklore, women's studies, and comparative literature; and the journals of The American Folklore Society, The Tennessee Folklore Society, and many other organizations. I found that uniquely American myths, legends, folktales, and tall tales concerning heroic females *did* exist among many groups within American society. For the most part, they were simply not well known. And there are a number of books that gather women-centered folk and fairy tales; but they include relatively few stories from the United States.

Why did these characters fail to achieve the fame of their male counterparts? In the past, American society expected women to limit their concerns to home and family—not to put themselves forward as explorers, hunters, warriors, or rulers. Though real-life women claimed these roles, most storytellers (the majority of them men), whether creating with pen and paper or spinning a yarn around a camp fire, portrayed female characters—even the "outsize" wives of such figures as Paul Bunyan—as pretty much content to stick close to home, play a supporting role, and let the menfolk have the real adventures. It was unusual to have a woman pictured as a huntress in her own right (not merely as someone who cleaned her husband's kill), or a powerful leader, a war chief, a cunning trickster, or a hero who rescued men from monsters.

Tales of such women went against popular thinking and made people uncomfortable. So they were not often told. There were exceptions: the stories of the fire goddess, Pele, and her sister, Hiiaka, are popular, enduring Hawaiian myths. For many Native American peoples, stories of warrior women have remained an important part of their heritage.

But even the overlooked heroines have simply been biding their time:

they are too vital—their stories too full of excitement, humor, and courage—to languish forever on the shelf. In the pages that follow, you will meet some of these too-long-ignored characters. Here are females of power from Anglo American, African American, Spanish American, and Native American traditions. These are women who controlled the power of fire and lightning (Hiiaka and Pale-Faced Lightning); women who were giant-slayers (Hekeke and Old Sally Cato); "sisters under the fur" (Molly Hare and Sister Fox), who are every bit as spunky and clever as their counterpart, Br'er Rabbit; and women who were strong enough to triumph over the heat and thirst of alkali deserts along the California trail (Sweet Betsey) or the cold and near-starvation of the Arctic winter (Otoonah).

This gathering is merely a start. I could not include all the tales of all the bigger-than-life American women I encountered; but I am confident that others will continue to bring to light more stories of heroines cut from the same cloth.

*Robert D. San Souci*
*Albany, California, 1992*

# Introduction

WOMEN OF WONDER, WOMEN OF POWER

THEY HAVE BEEN here all along, these American women of wonder, women of power. They have been tilling the soil, shearing the sheep, spinning and weaving, and working the land. They have shot game and given birth, cut logs for the fire, sewn the shrouds for their neighbors, hoed and hewed and harvested. But silently.

Too silently.

We have all helped make them mute, forgetting to tell their magic stories or, even worse, gifting their fathers and brothers and sons with their heroic deeds.

Robert San Souci is one of a hardy band of pioneers who have been rescuing the silent women, giving them back their tongues. Sometimes those voices speak the language of the indigenous peoples—the Chippewa, Seneca, Miwok, Pueblo. Sometimes those voices speak the language of the Europeans who brought their stories across the ocean in the lower decks. Sometimes those voices are the voices of slaves carried in chains from Africa to the American shore.

Why is it important to hear these women's wonder tales? Because women as well as men can be intelligent, inventive, brave. Heroism is not a gender-driven activity. And because to keep silent in the face of such heroism is to deny it ever existed.

So give welcome to Annie Christmas and Molly Cottontail, and the larger-than-life Sal Fink. Meet Sister Fox and Otoonah and Hiiaka, who battled demons and death itself to rescue her beloved. These are truly women of wonder, women of power.

Women who are no longer mute.

*—Jane Yolen*

# La Sauvagesse

**THE GIRL OF THE WILDS**

*Je suis du bord de l'Ohio.*
I am from the banks of the Ohio.
*J'ai le courage pour noblesse.*
I have a heart for great deeds
*Ma joie est d'être à mon canot,*
My joy is to be in my canoe,
*De la guider avec adresse.*
To guide it skillfully.
*Ma vie est la chasse et la pêche.*
My life is to hunt and to fish.
*Enfin, je suis la Sauvagesse,*
Yes, I am the girl of the wilds,
(Chorus) *Tou ratatou ratoura,*
*Tou ratatou ratoura.*

*—Folk song sung by French explorers
in the Louisiana Territory
in the 1800s*

# Women of the Northeast

# The Star Maiden

## CHIPPEWA

The Chippewa are part of the Ojibwa people who settled in the region of the Great Lakes and upper Mississippi. Tribal legends suggest that the people originated on the Atlantic seaboard but followed a magic shell inland to what was a land of plenty: a region of forests rich with elk and deer, and shallow lakes where wild rice grew.

The tale that follows has parallels in widespread legends of swan maidens and seal maidens told in the Middle East, Far East, Europe, the Caribbean, and elsewhere. Such beings—usually, but not always, female—are visitors from other realms (mysterious lands under seas, lakes, or distant islands) who are compelled to live among humans when their means of returning to their place of origin is lost through human trickery. Often it is the loss of a magical garment that transforms the being into creature of sea or sky.

ONE DAY, WHILE hunting on the prairie beyond the forest, Algon, a young hunter, discovered a circle of beaten earth in the midst of the tall grass—it looked as though it had been worn by the tread of feet in a round dance. Nowhere else outside the edge of the circle could he find footprints. Filled with curiosity, he hid himself in the grass to see what sort of dancers could come to the circle without leaving any trace.

Very soon, he heard women chanting—their voices faint and sweet and seeming to come from high up in the air. Looking to the sky, Algon saw a faint pale speck descending, like a bit of midday moon falling to earth. As it came nearer, the singing grew clearer. Now he recognized it as an ancient song of power such as those used by the medicine elder of his tribe.

Earth!
Mother!
From the sky-place
We come to honor you!
Your bowl is always full of food and water
To nourish all the people!
Your green blanket is spread wide
To shelter all living beings!
Earth!
Mother!
We come to honor you!

Nearer and nearer the pale thing came. Now he could see that it was a huge magic basket woven of willow branches. Inside, twelve young women leaned upon the rim, gazing out over prairie and forest. They sang, and the basket dropped gently into the center of the circle of packed earth. Climbing out, they began to dance around and around. As they danced, Algon felt a great power gathering around them; it took all his courage not to run away from the strangers who commanded such power.

Now, each of the women was beautiful, tall and graceful, with sleek, raven-colored hair and shining eyes. They were so much alike that the man guessed at once that they were sisters. But the youngest seemed the most radiant of all. Seeing her, Algon felt consumed with love. Stepping from his hiding place in the tall grass, he approached the circle. He hoped to speak to the young woman, find out who she was, and tell her of the love he felt.

But at the sight of the young man, the sky women climbed into the willow basket. In a moment they were singing, and it rose up into the air with the magic they commanded. For a brief time, the heartbroken young man heard their sweet voices. Then the sound faded, and sadly he returned to his lodge.

Try as he might, Algon could not get the Star Maiden's face out of his mind. Every time he set out to hunt deer, he found himself drawn back to the dancing circle on the prairie. For days on end, he sat behind a screen of tall grass, hoping to hear the young woman's voice and glimpse her face again.

At last the willow basket with the twelve sky maidens drifted slowly to earth, accompanied by the women's songs of power. Again the twelve danced a round dance, while Algon watched.

Finally, he stepped forward, his hands outstretched with palms up to show that he meant them no harm. "Please do not be afraid," he said. All but the youngest drew back. Instead, she stepped forward boldly, saying to her sisters, "This person has an honest face. Perhaps he wants to teach us his earthly dances."

But the other sky women would not hear of this. The eldest said, "Our father has told us that we may visit Mother Earth, but he has forbidden us to speak with humans. My sister, climb into the basket with us now so that we may go home."

The youngest woman hesitated, as though she might disobey. Then she sighed and did as she was told. Swiftly they rose from sight, while Algon stretched his arms vainly up to the sky.

Algon returned home more miserable than ever. All night long he lay awake, thinking of the pretty, unapproachable creature who had so captivated him. At the first light of dawn, he went yet again to the enchanted spot, hoping that some idea would present itself to him.

At one end of the circle was a hollow log in which a family of mice had made their home. Gradually a plan came to mind. He would beg the medicine elder to change him into a mouse. He would hide in the log. Then, while the sisters were dancing, he would hide himself in their basket. When they reached the sky land from which they came, he would change himself back to a man and plead with the maiden to become his wife.

In return for much dried meat, the medicine elder gave Algon a medicine bag. "Wear this around your neck," the old woman said, "and touch it when you want to take that other shape. When you wish to become a man again, you will become as you were."

So Algon went a final time to the circle of beaten earth. When he spotted the willow basket descending, he touched his medicine bag and turned himself into a mouse and hid in the hollow log.

When the basket had settled to the ground, all but the youngest sister looked around fearfully, unwilling to get out until they were sure that no one was watching them. The youngest sister watched also, but Algon thought that her look was one of longing.

Thinking that they were alone, one by one the twelve got out and began to sing and dance joyfully. But several times the youngest stepped into the tall grass outside the dancing circle. She eagerly noted the flicker of a gray squirrel in the treetops and the flash of a blue jay overhead. Her eldest sister had to call her back into the circle each time.

Algon waited for the best moment to hide himself in the basket. Suddenly, the eldest sister stopped the others in mid-step. "Now, I do not think that we are alone here," she said.

"Sister, there is nothing but that old log here," said the second-oldest maiden. Surely that is no danger to us. See!" she said, giving the log a push with her foot, so that the mice inside scampered in all directions, "there are only some mice."

But the sharp eyes of the youngest sister saw that one mouse had not run for the tall grass but was trying to reach the basket. Gently she plucked up the mouse and held it in her palm, looking at it curiously.

Then she walked to the edge of the circle and set it down beside the tall grass, thinking it would run away to join its fellows.

To her astonishment, Algon suddenly regained his own shape. He grabbed her hand and would not release her. "Please, I mean you no harm! Only talk to me," he begged.

Startled, she at first tried to draw back. Then she said, "Release me, and I will ask my sisters to stay here." But the man was so fearful that she would flee, he would not let go of her hand, although she tried to break free.

Now, at the unexpected sight of the human, the other women had climbed back into the basket. Although the youngest maiden pleaded with them to wait, her sisters, frightened that more of Algon's people might be in hiding and try to catch them, ascended swiftly to their star country.

At first the young woman grew angry at Algon. "If you had not held me so, I could have persuaded my sisters to remain here, for I am eager to stay for a time on the earth. But how am I to return home?" she demanded. For a while she sat angrily on the hollow log and refused to look at him. But when evening fell, and the tall grass and distant woods came alive with the calls of night-hunting birds and animals, she let Algon lead her back to his village of birch-bark wigwams in the shelter of the forest. Still she would not speak to him.

Once there, she refused to enter his lodge. To his sorrow Algon saw that tears as bright as the stars were flowing from her eyes.

As the woman stood gazing up at the shining stars, Algon began playing a flute. Its sweet music at last touched her heart. His love and kindness won her over, and she agreed to marry him.

In time, she bore him a son and learned the ways of his people, so that she hung spiderwebs on the hoop of the baby's cradle board to catch any harm in the air and made a mouthwash of bark and roots to help her son when he was teething.

People said what a good wife and mother she was. Although Star

Maiden loved her husband and child, a part of her always longed to return to her home in the heavens.

While she remained happy in her marriage, the desire to see her sky home and sisters grew too much to bear. By chance, she came upon a willow whose twigs were the same kind used to make the basket in which she had first come to earth. Quickly she gathered armful after armful of the small branches and carried them to the magic circle. There she wove them into a second, smaller basket.

When it was completed, she took her little son and gifts of moccasins embroidered with porcupine quills, flowers, and wild rice for the star people. Then, seating herself in the basket, she sang one of the songs of power that she still remembered. In this way, she called upon the great *manitou,* who is the most powerful being of all:

> Oh, Great Spirit, hear my prayer,
> Oh, Great Spirit, hear my prayer,
> Raise this basket to the night sky,
> And return me to my father.

Then she shook a large gourd rattle. Chanting all the time, she caused the willow basket to float up to her father's sky realm. There she was greeted warmly by her father and sisters.

Algon grieved bitterly for his lost wife and child. He begged the medicine elder to help him find a way to follow them, but she could not help. Every day he would go to the magic circle on the prairie and raise his arms to the sky and pray to be reunited with his loved ones.

In her happiness at being back in her own land, the Star Maiden almost forgot Algon and the green-mantled earth. But soon enough, she was sure that she could hear his voice calling to her from far below. And her little boy asked often for his father.

Although her heart was torn at the thought of leaving the star land again, the Star Maiden could bear the cries of her little boy no more. So at last she chose to return to Algon.

She went to her father, although she feared he would be displeased by her decision. "My father, though what I must ask will fill your heart with anger as surely as it breaks my heart, I beg you to let me return to Mother Earth. There I will live out my days in my husband's lodge."

But the sky ruler, impressed by his daughter's courage and touched by her love, said to her, "Bring Algon with you so that all of you can live in this place. But when you return, you must bring some bit of every beast and bird you can find."

So it was that Algon, who spent most of his time in the center of the magic circle, saw his wife and son coming back to him in the bigger willow basket. Happy to be reunited with them, he willingly agreed to go and live with them in the star country.

The Star Maiden led her husband and child in a search to gather traces of as many animals and birds as they could. When they had collected the objects—a claw, a feather, a shell, a fishscale, and so on—they piled these in the willow basket. Then the three climbed in themselves, and the Star Maiden's song carried them back up to the star country.

There, her father gathered all his people in front of his great lodge. At his direction, the Star Maiden and Algon placed the relics they had brought upon a blanket decorated with beadwork showing all the animals of the earth. The young woman and young man were careful to set each feather or tuft of fur or fishscale upon the picture of the animal from which it came.

When they had finished, the ruler spoke. "Choose one object from those you see here," he invited each sky-person. "It will give you the power to become that creature. This is my daughter's gift to you."

One by one, the people took the relics, changing into the animal or bird they wished to be. At the very end, three feathers of a white falcon were left upon the blanket. The Star Maiden took these for herself and her family. In this way, they were able to fly down and return to the prairies and forests whenever they wanted to.

And, legends say, their descendents may still be seen from time to time in the form of snow-white falcons.

# Bess Call

## ANGLO AMERICAN

Joe Call, who lived in Essex County, New York, until his death in 1834, was reported to be the strongest man in America. Joe is a beloved hero among the mountains and hills of the Adirondacks. . . . There was said to have been a very powerful Call sister who was hardly second to Joe in physical prowess, Bess Call. She is a favorite of storytellers.

STRONGMAN JOE CALL had a sister, Bess, who was also as big as life and twice as natural. She was younger than he was, a little shorter (not quite six feet tall), but just as sturdy. She was as broad as a Dutch barn and had double joints and a double set of teeth—just like Joe. Stories say that she was as handsome as her brother was plain, having eyes as blue as whetstones and hair as black as a stack of black cats in the dark.

Now Bess usually gave the appearance of being as calm as a pan of skim milk. But, when they were young, Bess had been the terror of the neighborhood bullies who tormented smaller children or helpless animals. Just let her spot a ruffian taking sweets from a toddler or tying a can to a dog's tail: she would squeeze up her face and curl her hands into fists and bellow, "Leave off what you're doin', or I'm gonna thrash you within an inch o' your life!" Those who chose to stand their ground soon found that Bess had the brawn to back her threat.

"That's not ladylike!" people would scold, pointing to her scuffed shoes and torn pinafore—trophies of her most recent battle.

But Bess just shrugged off such carping and went her own way, as independent as a hog on ice.

"If I'da been born in olden times," she would tell her brother, "you wouldn't find me sittin' around a castle bein' ladylike—wearin' a pointy hat and pinin' for some prince t'come lookin' for me. I'd fetch me some gold armor and go fight dragons and wicked kings and such ever' day."

Joe was different: he liked wrestling for the fun of it. For a time, he traveled throughout the world, engaging in wrestling matches one after the other. But as he got a bit older, he grew more settled in his ways. So one day he and Bess bought a farm and put all their efforts into making the place a roaring success.

But day after day, one by one, young men traipsed out to challenge Joe, even though he had long since finished with wrestling. Sometimes he could talk them out of it; sometimes there was nothing for it but for Joe to just pin them and send them packing.

One hot summer morning, a wrestler rode out on horseback to the Calls' hometown of Lewis. Across the sea in England, he had heard of Joe's prowess and had come to challenge the "Lewis Giant," as Joe had come to be known.

He came upon Joe, who had paused to take a breather while plowing a field. At that moment, Joe had halted the team of oxen so that he could jaw with Bess, who had just finished splitting a cord of wood into kindling. As they talked he downed a jug of lemonade.

Because he had never met Joe, the stranger paused and asked, "Sir, could you direct to the Call homestead?"

Still drinking lemonade, Joe lifted his huge plow and pointed toward the farmhouse down the road a piece.

The man's face fell. "I believe you must be Joe Call," he said weakly. Joe nodded.

"Well," said the stranger, "I came here hoping to have a match with you, but I think, perhaps, this is not the best day for it."

14

"It's hotter'n Hannah," Joe agreed.

At this, the hopeful champion turned tail and galloped back toward town. As she watched him go, Bess grinned and said, "That feller's face looked long enough to eat oats out of a churn." After a minute, she lifted up the plow, pointed to the blade, and said to her brother, "This is gettin' mighty dull. I'll sharpen it when you're finished plowin' t'night."

It turned out that the Britisher hadn't skedaddled back across the Atlantic. Instead, he went and hired himself a trainer and worked and worked to beef up his muscles until he, too, could lift a plow with one hand. By midsummer, he could hold it steady at arm's length for a full minute, and so he felt himself ready to challenge the "Lewis Giant," fair and square.

This time he chanced upon Joe and Bess one evening as they were leading the oxen to the barn.

He politely wished them "Good evening."

" 'Evenin'," brother and sister answered. "What brings you back this way?"

"Well . . . that is . . . I had hoped. . ."

"Say what you got to plunk and plain," said Bess. "There's some folks as has chores t'do."

"Well, ma'am," he said, "I've come to challenge your brother to a wrestling match."

"Save yourself some trouble and bruises, mister," said Bess. "Joe ain't interested in wrestling with someone so thin I'd have to shake the sheets to find you."

The Britisher flexed his new muscles angrily, saying, "I think you'd better let your brother speak his mind."

"It's your funeral," Bess said.

"Don't know that I have the time for such foolishness," said Joe. "The ox here was slow. Didn't get done half what I wanted." He lifted the beast, which weighed more than eight hundredweight, over his head with one hand and said to Bess, "See if there's somethin' wrong with that right front hoof."

"Sure is," said his sister. "That shoe is near split in two, and there's a rock caught in between." She removed the rock, then told her brother, "Set'm down, and I'll help you shoe'm in the mornin'."

Then they remembered the English wrestler; but when they looked around, they saw him charging away down the road.

"He's mighty flighty, that foreigner," said Bess. Then she lifted the other ox over her head. "Best check the shoes on this one, too, while we're at it."

But the challenger did not go home this time, either. He went back to town and hired two trainers and worked and worked to build up his strength, until he, too, could lift an ox with one hand spread flat under its barrel. By the end of summer, he could keep an ox aloft while one of his trainers clocked off a full five minutes on his pocket watch.

Then, feeling that he was finally ready to wrestle Joe Call, the man rode out to the farm. He tied his horse to the hitching post near the porch and swaggered up the front steps.

That day, however, Joe was not at home. Through the half-open Dutch door, the young man saw Bess sitting in her parlor, bending and unbending a horseshoe fretfully.

Surprised at this, but unwilling to go away without his match, the fellow politely asked if he could wait for Joe. Although she was feeling out of sorts and as cranky as a sore-headed bear, Bess invited him in.

"Joe won't return until this evenin'," she said by way of making conversation.

"I'll wait, if I may," the man said. "I have come all the way from England just to wrestle with him."

"I usually do the wrestlin' while Joe's away," said Bess. "You pin me once or twice, an' I'll say you're fit for a match with my brother."

The man chuckled, thinking she was making a joke. At the sound of his laugh, the horseshoe in her big hands snapped in two.

Now, Bess was a lot like her brother—they could both be dangerous when angry. Realizing that he wasn't about to take her seriously—and even madder to see him *laughing* at her—Bess seized her visitor by the slack of his pants and threw him through the upper half of the open door out into the front yard.

"Since I was knee-high to a katydid," she said, dusting off her hands, "nothin' has riled me more'n some fellow thinkin' he's better 'cause I'm female. Makes me mad enough t' jump down his throat and swing on his tonsils!"

The would-be wrestler arose, slapped the dust off his trousers, and made an obliging bow. "I stand corrected," he said. "I'll wrestle you. It will be excellent practice for the *real* match, when your brother comes home."

"Humph!" said Bess. "I'll show you a *'real match'*—and no waitin', neither." She rolled up her sleeves and stomped out into the yard.

Back and forth they tussled, making more noise than a boatload of calves on the Hudson. First one, and then the other seemed to get the upper hand, only to find that the edge had slipped over to his or her opponent. The cloud of dust they kicked up covered the sun so that people as far away as Clinton and Cayuga counties reached for their umbrellas thinking unseasonable rain was about to fall.

Their struggles sent them rolling across the yard right up to the fence that separated the farmyard from the road. There Bess took hold of the Englishman one last time and tossed him body, boots, and britches over the fence, where he landed in a muddy ditch.

Standing up with as much dignity as he could muster, the man began to scrape the mud off his shirt and pants. At the same time he said, "If you will kindly throw me my horse, I will start for home, now."

"Happy t'oblige," said Bess. Over went his horse, too.

So it was that Joe, returning from town, was passed by the mud-splattered visitor riding away at full gallop.

"What happened to that English fellow?" asked Joe, when he reached the house.

"Oh, I showed him who's the better wrestler," said Bess with a smile. "He's pretty poor potatoes—and a sore loser, t'boot. I didn't have the heart t'tell him that I've been feelin' a mite under the weather."

"Well," said her brother, "maybe he'll come back for a rematch when you're feelin' stronger."

"If he thinks he'll *ever* get the better of me," Bess said with a laugh, "he has brass enough in his head t'make a five-pound kettle—and sap enough inside t'fill it."

But the would-be champion was smart enough to keep riding until he reached New York City. There he he booked passage home to England, where he stayed, having sworn off wrestling for the rest of his days.

# Drop Star

## ANGLO AMERICAN

In upstate New York, the Native Americans who inhabited the Genesee River area were the Seneca, members of the Iroquois Confederacy. The Drop Star story common to that area does not specify the tribe to which old Skenandoh, the last of his people, belonged. They might well have been Mahican, a group originally inhabiting the Upper Hudson Valley in New York, with a branch in Connecticut—the latter were later known as Mohegans.

Although this story includes details of life in the two tribes mentioned, "Drop Star" appears to be a local account popularized by the white settlers who moved into the region. It falls under the heading of "place legends"—those connected with a particular place or explaining how some local feature or area was named. The story that follows may include some historical truth, but now it has grown and changed with each retelling so that it would be difficult to sift fact from fiction.

IN A REMOTE cabin on the Genesee River, three-year-old Charlotte lived with her widowed mother. The Senecas, who lived in the area, called her "Kayutah," or "Drop Star," because her skin seemed as pale and shining as an earthbound star. The child had a tiny round, red birthmark, like a berry, near her throat.

As small as she was, she worked hard helping her mother by doing small chores indoors or weeding the vegetable garden at the front of the cabin. She was also a fiercely independent child, who often did whatever she wanted to without stopping to think.

One day, Charlotte decided to gather water lilies from the little nearby lake as a gift to surprise her mother. She forgot her mother's warning that she must never go to the shore alone. Humming to herself, she used a stick to pull the lilies close to shore. She was so caught up in her work that she did not even look up when a shadow fell across her as she knelt in the mud, straining to reach the most perfect lily that floated just beyond reach of her stick.

Just after finishing her morning chores, Charlotte's mother discovered that the girl was neither in the cabin nor in the garden outside. Recalling that her daughter had asked to go and gather water lilies, the woman hurried to the lake. She called the child's name, but Charlotte did not answer. At first angry, then frightened, the frantic mother began running up and down the shore.

She searched and searched near a cluster of lilies by the water's edge but could find no trace of the child. The grieving women knew the settlers had driven out the dangerous black bear, gray wolf, and bobcat that had once lived near the lake. The Senecas had retreated farther and farther back into the wilderness. All that she could imagine was that her daughter had drowned.

Many years passed, and the woman remained in the little cabin. Often she would walk beside the lake, weeping softly as she stared at the drifting white water lilies.

Then, one day, a hunter, a stranger to her, came to the door of her house, now on the edge of a growing town. She knew at once that he was a Seneca, because of his doeskin kilt, leggings, moccasins, and cap with a single feather standing upright. A sash of red-and-blue broadcloth crisscrossed his chest.

"What do you want?" she asked him.

In the woman's language, the man said, "I have been sent by an old man, a Mahican named Skenandoh, who is the last of his tribe. I came to his lodge when I was hunting far to the west of where my own people live. He begged me to carry a message to you. I am to say to you, 'The ice is broken, and Skenandoh knows of a hill of snow where a red berry grows that will be yours, if you claim it.' "

"What does that mean?" the woman asked.

"Those were the words Skenandoh gave me. He did not tell me what was the meaning. He said that, if you were the right person, you would understand."

The woman asked him more questions, but the Seneca could tell her no more. At last, she gave him food and a few coins to thank him for his trouble.

Puzzled, she walked back and forth along the margin of the lake, trying to guess what the words meant. At first, nothing occurred to her. Suddenly, gazing at a mass of white lilies drifting on the still blue water, she cried out the name "Charlotte" as she grasped the meaning of the riddle. Her surprise was so great, she nearly fainted.

Her mind's eye showed her clearly the tiny red birthmark on her daughter's fair skin—so like "a hill of snow where a red berry grows." Surely, the old man had been telling her, by way of the young hunter, that her daughter still lived, and that the woman might claim her. Desperately, she ran through the town, seeking the young Seneca. When she found him, she asked, "Did you see a child—no, a young woman now—when you met the old man?"

He shook his head. "I saw only the man."

Then she asked him for careful directions of how to find Skenandoh. Listening to what he told her, she realized that a vast amount of wilderness separated her from her lost child.

Fearing that setting out alone would doom her search to failure, the

23

woman sent for a distant cousin to accompany her. Though her young relative did not arrive until sunset on the second day, the eager mother insisted that they set off at once.

They rode as swiftly as they could, over dim trails, with only stars for light. When the man begged for a few moments rest, she allowed him only the briefest nap before insisting that they continue on their way. They kept on riding hard, with only short pauses to rest themselves and their horses, or wolf down a bit of food.

In the gray light of dawn, several days later, they discovered a human skeleton, leaning against a tree, almost as if it were guarding the trail. At the sight of this, the woman pressed her hand to her throat. She looked away.

But her companion said gently, "This has been here a long time. It has nothing to do with our Charlotte."

The horrible marker had given them a new sense of urgency. Spurring the horses on at breakneck speed, the two raced over the hills that bordered Lake Seneca. Then, following the directions that the hunter had given her, the woman led the way as they struck even deeper into the wilds.

For a time, they found no further traces of people. Then they came upon several old fish dams in a stream, indicating that some tribe had visited the area within recent memory.

At last, when horses and riders were near collapse, they reached a small lake. Nearly falling from their saddles, the two of them discovered a wigwam of elm bark on the shore of the lake. Baskets for corn planting and berrying were scattered beside the lodge, and nets of woven vines had been set out to dry on stones near the water. The woman's cousin pointed to the fox totem carved in the wood above the door. "That's a clan sign," he said. "Whoever lives here must be an important man, perhaps a *sachem*, chief."

But the woman only made a distressed sound as she pointed to a freshly dug grave a short distance from the lodge, at the edge of a small corn field.

"Perhaps we've come too late," said the young man, putting his arm around her shoulder.

At that instant, an aged man, his face drawn and wrinkled but his eyes still bright, stepped out of the wigwam. He was wrapped in a doeskin robe. For a moment, the three stared at one another in silence.

At last, the woman asked in a shaking voice, "Are you Skenandoh?"

The old man nodded.

"I have come to claim the berry that springs from the snow," she said. Her voice quavered, and she could not keep her eyes from the new grave.

"You come in time," said Skenandoh. "That is not Kayutah's grave. My own daughter sleeps under the earth. She was as a sister to Kayutah, when I stole her away from you. But when my child grew ill, she made me promise to return Drop Star to her people." Looking sadly at the grave, he said, "I have kept my word."

Stepping into the wigwam, he emerged again, holding the hand of a girl of eighteen summers. She was dressed in a skirt and blouse of buckskin and soft moccasins with beaded flowers and berries. With head bowed, the slender, fair-haired young woman showed her mother the red birthmark, like a berry, near her pale throat.

The woman rushed forward to embrace her daughter. And their cousin wrapped his arms around both of them.

"Now I must go into the setting sun," said the old man, "to find my true daughter."

Before the others realized what he was doing, he had stepped into his elm-bark canoe at the water's edge, put a deerskin pouch around his neck that was filled with heavy stones, and paddled out to the middle of the lake.

For a time he sat singing songs in the language of his people, who had passed—all but him—from the land. Suddenly, he took a heavy ball-headed war club carved from a single piece of hardwood and smashed through the bottom of the frail canoe.

While the onlookers cried out in horror—Drop Star most loudly of all—the canoe filled with water. In a few moments, old Skenandoh had vanished from sight.

Then Drop Star and the others returned to the little cabin on the Genessee. There, with her mother's help, she learned the ways of her people; but, in her heart, she treasured both her lives. In time, Charlotte married the cousin who had helped rescue her.

And the lake that they lived beside came to be called Kayutah, or Drop Star.

# Women of the South

# Molly Cottontail

## AFRICAN AMERICAN

Molly Cottontail, or Molly Hare, is the female counterpart of Br'er Rabbit, who came to life in the well-known stories told by Joel Chandler Harris. Stories about her are related by Aunt Nancy (a play on "Anansi," the spider figure of Caribbean folklore) and Aunt 'Phrony to children visiting a plantation house in southern Virginia one year after the end of the Civil War.

Molly Cottontail's story has a parallel in the tale "Mr. Rabbit Nibbles Up the Butter," in *Uncle Remus: His Songs and His Sayings*. But it also appears throughout the Caribbean and Sea Islands in tales grouped under the heading of "The Theft of Butter," involving the characters of Boukee and Rabby—sometimes human brothers, sometimes animals.

Molly's stories, as printed in Anne Virginia Culbertson's *At the Big House*, represent a refreshing and lively look at the clever, antic rabbit.

---

"AUNT NANCY," SAID little Janey, who was sitting in the big kitchen of the plantation house, "do you know any more stories about Miss Molly Cottontail? I think she's almost as smart as Mr. Hare, and I like to hear about her almost as much."

"Almos' as smart!" said Nancy, throwing up her hands in surprise. "Let me tell you that when a woman start out to be trickish she can beat a man every time, 'cause her mind works a heap faster. She see all 'round and over and underneath and on both sides of a thing." To show what she meant, Aunt Nancy darted her head every which way, like a hen on the lookout for chicks and worms and weasels and chicken hawks at the same time. "Meanwhile, a man's just tryin' to stare plumb through it." And she stared at Janey with such a wide-eyed, moon-calf look, the little girl began to giggle.

Then Janey asked, "Why is she called Miss Molly Cottontail and not Mrs. Hare, when she's married to Mr. Hare?"

To this, Aunt Nancy replied, "I know she's called Miss Molly Cottontail because she never fancied herself just wholly and solely the wife of Mistah Hare. She ain't the sort of female to settle down and be just plain 'Missus Hare' all her days, and stay home and listen to the children cry and wash their faces and comb their hair and cook their vittles, year in and year out. Miss Molly, she got too much git-up in her for that. She make Old Man Hare stay home and mind the children now and then— and he don't dast say no, neither."

"Oh, *please* tell me a story about Molly," Janey begged.

"All I can say is you got to be the persistentest child I ever run into!" said Aunt Nancy. All the while kneading bread dough for the family's supper, the woman began the tale.

One day Miss Molly and Mistah Fox went to visit Mistah Fox's brother, who lived across the swamp and down in the holler. He was called Hungry Billy, 'cause he was all the time eatin' up folkses' chickens. Molly was all dressed up in her fancy hat and shawl and her good manners, goin' along makin' herself mighty agreeable with chitchat and little jokes.

When the two reached Hungry Billy's house, Molly put her hat and shawl and handbag on the bed. Then she offered to cook supper, exclaimin', "I kain't bear ter be idle even when I'se off on a visit."

So she fixed pine-bag tea and ash cakes. While she was workin', Billy brought her a pot of butter to help with the cookin'. Molly, who loved butter more than anything else, said, "Dat's a mighty 'pressive lot o' butter you got dere. How do you keep hit from spoilin' on such a waum day?"

"I set dat down in de stream, where hit cool," Billy told her. Then he put the butter pot back, while Molly watched through the window.

After they had eaten their ash cakes and tea, Billy went off to run an errand and Mistah Fox dozed by the fire. But Molly took herself to the stream and lifted the stone crock of butter out of the water. At first, she was only gonna take a bite, but that butter just tasted sweeter with every mouthful. Soon her greediness got the better of her. She ate up all the butter before she was sensible of what she was doing.

Straightaway she put the empty butter jar back in the water and hightailed it back to the house.

A short time later, when Mistah Fox woke up, he found Miss Molly sittin' on a chair, lookin' as innocent as a lamb, goin' on with her knittin' and hummin' a sweet little tune, just as if she never had butter on her mind or in her mouth.

Soon after this, Billy returned. His guests told him good-bye, and went back to their homes.

Next morning, Billy discovered that his butter crock was as empty as a sucked egg. He went first to Mistah Fox and then to Molly Hare and demanded, "Which o' you went and et up my butter? De crock as clean ez if hit been scoured."

Both said, " 'Twan't me." And Molly added, "'Deed, what I want wid you' butter anyway? I got plenty o' butter at home. Plus, I got a mighty delercate stomach. I kain't eat no butter 'lessen I done churned it myself, 'cause I kain't be sure other folks been right clean and careful in de makin'."

This made Billy even madder, and he spluttered out, "Well, mebbe my butter wasn't so *clean:* I dunno 'bout dat. But I does know 'bout this: Hit *clean gone.* What's mo', one er you two is de th'ef who goned it."

Then Billy, who was the biggest fox around, raised himself up to his full size and showed Molly Cottontail and Mistah Fox his teeth.

"I'se gonna keep you bofe right yer," he said, " 'til one er you 'fess up."

But Molly said to Billy, "You let Mistah Fox 'n' me lay down yonner in de waum sun all day. De heat er de sun gonna draw de butter right out de skin er who done et de butter."

"I don' know 'bout dat," said Hungry Billy doubtfully.

"It de truf," said Molly, "Anyone kin tell you dat—it jest coinkidenkal dat I'm de one ter remind you er dis nat'ral fac'."

"How kin you remin' me what I didn' know afore now?" Billy wondered.

"Well, now you know," said Molly Cottontail with a nod of her head. "Next time, when someone remind you er dis t'ing, you kin 'member, 'cause I jest told you so."

"I don' know ef I follers all dat," said Billy, scratchin' his head.

"Hit real simple," said Molly, talkin' slow, "Mistah Fox an' me, we sleep in de sun. You go 'long 'bout yo' bizness. When you git back, all you gots ter do is rub yo' fingers over our stummicks. Dat sun will draw out de butter and slick de fur er someone I kin name"—here she looked meaningfully at Mistah Fox—"only I ain't gone ter go 'cusin' someone widout proof. Den you'll know in a jiff who done et yo' butter."

"All right, I s'ppose," said Billy, settlin' down to watch Miss Molly, Mistah Fox, and the sun.

"No, no, no!" cried Miss Molly. "You got ter go 'bout yo' bizness, 'cause it take a *long* time fo' de sun ter draw out dat butter."

"I ain' *got* no bizness," Billy protested.

"De only bizness you ain't got is 'cusin' innercent people like me o' thievery. What bizness you is got is what you find yourself doin' when you git outta here so's you kin do hit."

Billy might have asked for her to explain that more. But somehow Miss Molly's clarifyin' only seemed to muddy the waters. With a sigh, Billy went off to find what business he was gonna meet up with.

Then Miss Molly pretended to fall asleep, while Mistah Fox—his mind innocent of this particular crime—really *did* fall asleep. As soon as Hungry Billy was out of sight and Mistah Fox was snorin' away, Molly went to her larder, took the last bit of her own butter, and smeared it over the sleepin' fox's stomach so softly that he didn't feel it. Then she licked her paws clean and laid down in her place again, pretendin' to fall asleep herself.

When Hungry Billy returned and found the butter on the speechless fox's fur, he began to accuse his cousin of being a thief.

At that moment, Miss Molly Cottontail began to stretch and rub her eyes and pretend like she just woke up. She listened to all the arguin' for a few minutes, and then she commenced to say, "Laws-a-mussy! I wouldn' believe dis if I ain' seen hit wid my own eyes. I'm certainly scannelize' dat a friend er mine took to stealin'—and mos' 'specially, on a perlite visit. I declare to goodness my feelin's is so hurted dat I kain' rightly 'spress myse'f. What's mo', I kain' stay here 'sociatin' wid a common th'ef. I gots my innercent young family ter think 'bout."

And off she scooted, while the foxes kept accusin' each other of all manner of crimes.

"So it turned out," Aunt Nancy told little Janey, "a coolness sprung up in that fox family that lasted for a lotta years. And it was all on account o' that crock of butter."

Then the woman shook her head, saying, "I tell you, child, that it don't take much to start a family quarrel, but it takes a heap of time and trouble to patch one up—just the same as it do with the holes where your brother Ned snags his britches. And those britches never do seem the same after the patchin', neither."

# Annie Christmas

## AFRICAN AMERICAN

Annie Christmas is cut from the same cloth as John Henry, Paul Bunyan, or Pecos Bill. Stories had it that she lived in New Orleans over a century ago, working as a longshoreman on the river docks near the French Quarter. She was six feet eight inches tall, black as coal, weighed over 250 pounds, and was fearless—especially when it came to dealing with bullies who haunted the New Orleans river docks. Rumor said that she could carry a barrel of flour under each arm, with another balanced on her head. To be called "as strong as Annie Christmas" was to be paid the best compliment going; her voice alone was as loud as a foghorn sounding upriver.

Annie—like Paul Bunyan and Pecos Bill—was first a literary creation, but she has passed (along with her brothers) into the folklore of the South.

The authors of *Gumbo Ya-Ya* (1945), the collection of Louisiana folktales in which Annie first appears, have this to say about her: ". . . longshoremen and all life on the riverfront are not what they used to be. It's gone soft now. . . . In other days men were really men, yet the toughest of them all was a woman." Anyone who didn't believe this only had to tangle with Annie once. She'd make him a believer in short order.

WHEN ANNIE CHRISTMAS wasn't working, she divided her time between fighting and gambling. That was how she won a keelboat. She would run the large, flat-bottomed boat—carrying cotton, sugar, tobacco, lumber, and passengers—down and *up* the river. This was unusual because only Annie was strong enough to pole and haul a keelboat upstream, against the current. For all other flatboats, the trip downriver to New Orleans was a one-way journey. When keelboats and broadhorns, arks and rafts reached the mouth of the Mississippi, they were broken up and sold for lumber. But not Annie's boat, which she christened *Big River's Daughter,* because both the boat, and herself, were true children of The Mississippi.

She sometimes dressed in a man's clothes but always wore a string of freshwater pearls to which she added one pearl every time she whipped a man in a fight. By the time she died, stories say, that necklace measured thirty feet. When pressed, she could beat a dozen men at a time. She is reported to have told even the ring-tailed roarer, Mike Fink, to stay on the upper Mississippi and not overstep himself by taking business on the lower part of the river—*her* territory. If he did, she said, "I'll whip him and send'm home lashed to his own keelboat!"

A widow, she had twelve sons, all born on the same day of the year. Each was as ebony-skinned as herself, handsome, and seven feet tall.

There were countless stories told about Annie up and down the Mississippi, from New Orleans to Natchez. Folks tell of the time the river got so high one winter that it threatened to flood the lowlands for miles about. Annie grew so impatient with the slow work of the men trying to build a barricade against the floodwaters that she raised the levee all by herself.

One day, Annie said to herself, "Law, I'm gettin' on in years. I gotta take things a bit easy."

So she dressed herself in a red satin dress, with matching red plumes in her hair. She invited a number of her lady friends to sail with her on a pleasure cruise up the Mississippi. But each time she docked, one of her friends would find herself a beau and stay on in the river town. By the time she reached Red River Landing, Annie found herself poling the keelboat alone.

When she spotted a magnificent steamboat, the *Natchez Belle*, getting ready to set sail, she decided to book passage and return to New Orleans on board the side-wheeler. Because she had spent most of her money, she thought she would have to go as a *standee*, a deck passenger, and stand and sit and sleep on deck, with only cotton bales and other cargo as furniture.

But she got to gambling with some of the dock workers and won honestly—and handsomely—from them. So she changed her plans, because now she could afford to sail like a grand lady aboard this floating palace. She tied her keelboat to the stern of the paddle wheeler, and reserved herself the finest stateroom—one with velvet curtains, Turkish carpets, and a gilded looking glass.

The *Natchez Belle* had painted paddle boxes over the wheels on both sides, a golden star that hung between her high-flying twin smokestacks, and a fancy steamboat gun that was fired on special occasions. But as grand as the ship was, her captain was a small-minded man. He disliked people for the fact that they weren't men like himself. But he knew Annie's reputation as a fighter, and he wisely stayed out of her way.

For her part, Annie contented herself playing poker with the ship's resident river gamblers. They sat around marble-topped tables in one of the huge public rooms, while elegant chandeliers swayed overhead, and Annie skinned them the way they usually fleeced poor immigrants and rich plantation owners alike.

Unhappily, the captain was as stubborn as he was mean. When the weather turned bad, he decided to save time returning to New Orleans by using a new cutoff—a channel cut across a bend in the Mississippi River.

Now Annie knew the river like the back of her hand—knew Big River's every shoal and mud flat. And she knew that the cutoff wasn't ready for traffic yet. She stormed up to the pilothouse perched high above the water and told the captain, "There are snags and sandbars and logs and stumps and what-all lyin' in wait there. Stay clear of the cutoff."

"I am captain of the *Natchez Belle!*" the man yelled at her. "I will pilot my craft as I see fit." Then he ordered her out of the pilothouse with curses.

"If we were dockside, I'd beat you flat as a flounder," said Annie, grabbing a fistful of necklace and clacking her pearls at the red-faced man. "But I ain't gonna risk the lives of yo' passengers any more'n you have already."

Then, with great dignity, she left the pilothouse and climbed down the rain-slick stairs to the hurricane deck. There she found her fellow passengers—men and women alike—hanging over the railing shielding their eyes against the driving wind and rain, and anxiously watching the swirling, churning river. Big River was serving up big trouble: the water was yellow with mud. Worse, it was filled with tree stumps and limbs that bobbed and vanished then thrust up like the claws of some water devil to scrape the sides of the steamboat or try to rip open her hull.

With a terrible crunch, the *Natchez Belle* ran aground on a sandbar. Above the wind and rain and cries of frightened passengers, Annie could hear the captain screaming orders in the pilothouse.

There was a sickening scraping sound as the steamboat, reversing itself, pulled off the sandbar, only to chew tail-end into another. As the ship canted suddenly to starboard, the bellows in the pilothouse grew even more frenzied. The passengers huddled together, certain that the *Natchez Belle* was doomed and that they were going to be swallowed up by the raging yellow water.

Once again, Annie fought her way up to the pilothouse. "Let me at that wheel," she cried. "Snags are thicker'n fiddlers in Hades here'-bouts. But it might be I can steer us back to the main channel. I know this river like the back of my black hand!"

But the captain, his brow glistening with sweat and his eyes gleaming with madness, drew his pistol and ordered her out of his pilothouse. "The devil take you, woman!" he cried.

"He's gonna take you first," she said, "but I'm gonna take as many folks t'safety as I can meantimes!"

So saying, she retreated to the main deck again. Then, taking hold of the rope that held her keelboat in tow, she began to pull her own craft closer. Time and again, the rain-soaked hemp slipped between her hands, but she managed to find purchase and finally drew the keelboat close enough for people to cross to it.

"Anyone who wants t'come with me, hop aboard! I'm turning back to the main channel."

At first, the passengers hesitated. Then one man and woman clambered onto *Big River's Daughter.* Quickly, the others followed. Soon the keelboat was riding dangerously low in the water.

"Come on!" Annie called to the *Natchez Belle*'s crew, but they held back out of fear of the captain's anger and pistol.

"I can't wait no longer!" she cried. Then she jumped onto the keelboat and cast off the tow rope. Poling herself, and assisted by some of the other men and women, she turned the smaller craft around and began fighting her way back to the main river channel.

Behind her, the straining *Natchez Belle* lurched free of the imprisoning sandbar only to hurtle forward onto another studded with tree limbs and other debris. In a trice, the steamboat's hull was broken open and flooded by the boiling, yellow water. The riverboat spun around once on top of the waves, as though it had escaped the hungry river; twice, then it was already half swallowed by the torrent; thrice—but there was nothing but the twin black funnels that opened like flowers at the top then disappearing beneath the water.

"Now pole like yo' lives depend on it!" Annie ordered. "'Cause they *do!*"

Together, they reached the safety of the main river channel. At that moment, the storm eased, the river calmed, and the passengers hugged Annie for saving their lives. She turned as red as her satin dress at all this outpouring of goodwill.

"Wasn't more than anyone with a lick of sense and an ounce o' spunk would have done," she said. Then she cried, "This boat's goin' too slow!"

While the others watched, she tied the tow rope around her waist and jumped onto the shore. Then she began pulling the keelboat, running in long, loping strides. The boat leaped forward so suddenly that the passengers had to hang on for dear life. Then they were fairly flying over the surface of the water, while Annie, in her red satin skirt and red hair plumes, hauled them along like some strange bird of passage.

They reached New Orleans in record time, and the story of Annie's boat pulling soon became another riverside legend. But Annie's greatest feat had overtaxed her heart. She took to her bed soon afterward and called her sons to her side. They stood weeping, six to a side, while she told them how she wanted to be buried, then bid each good-bye with a kiss.

Soon after this, she died.

On the next evening when no moon was shining, her body was placed in a coal-black coffin and driven to the wharf in a coal-black hearse drawn by six coal black horses. Her sons, dressed in elegant mourning suits, marched six and six beside her.

When they reached the riverfront near the French Quarter, Annie's coffin was placed on a coal black barge. Together, Annie's sons launched the barge downriver and out to sea, keeping watch, until the vessel and the coffin it carried had vanished forever into the night.

# Susanna and Simon

## AFRICAN AMERICAN

Originally included in *Daddy Jake, the Runaway: And Short Stories Told After Dark*, by Uncle Remus (Joel Chandler Harris), this narrative is a familiar pattern in world folklore. In a note to the original text, Harris comments that the story was told to one of his children by an African American storyteller named John Holder. He goes on to note, "I have since found a variant (or perhaps the original) in Theal's *Kaffir Folk-lore.*" Kaffirs are members of one of the Bantu-speaking tribes who live in South Africa.

Stories of a young person's (or young couple's) use of commonplace objects (needles, soap, moss, and such) that are magically transformed into barriers (mountains, lakes, forests, and so on) to delay and defeat pursuers (ogres, witches, wizards, and their like) are well known in Europe, Latin America, the Middle East, and among such Plains Indian tribes as the Cheyenne and Blackfeet.

THERE ONCE WAS a man who had a mighty pretty daughter named Susanna. She was so pretty that she had more sweethearts than a man has fingers and toes. But her daddy didn't like any of them. Still, they kept on coming around and pestering the household. By'n'by he gave word that any man who cleared six acres of land and rolled up the logs and piled up the brush in one day—that man could marry his daughter.

Of course, this seemed as easy as climbin' a greased pole with two baskets of eggs. So all the suitors dropped off, except a great big strapping fellow who looked strong enough to knock a steer down. This young man's name was Simon. He truly loved Susanna. But what was far more important, she loved him back.

Well, Simon went up to the gal's daddy, and said, "If anybody kin clean up dis yere land, I'm de one ter do it. Leastways, I'm gwine try mighty hard."

The old man just laughed and said, "Dat's fine by me. You start in de mornin'."

Just then, Susanna bustled in, saying, "I jes have ter fix a little sumpin' in de cubberd." But when her daddy wasn't looking, she took and kissed her hand and blew Simon a kiss. Then she nodded her head to signal her sweetheart that everything would turn out fine. That was all Simon needed. He went off as happy as a jaybird after he's robbed a sparrow's nest.

But there was trouble brewing, for Susanna's father was a witch. He could conjure anyone who wasn't wearing a rabbit's foot. Simon always wore a lucky rabbit's foot that his grandma had given him. So the man went away to study just what he could do if Simon cleared the land—unlikely as that seemed.

However, Susanna's pa had been working at his "conjurements" so long that Susanna had learned most of his tricks. The spunky girl—who was as clever as she was pretty—decided to take the matter of her future into her own hands.

So the next morning, when Simon came by the house to borrow an axe, Susanna ran and got it for him. When she did, she sprinkled some black sand on it and said, "Axe, cut; cut, axe." Then she rubbed her hair across it and gave it to Simon along with a little pouch made of red cloth. When he took both these things, Susanna said, "Go down by de crick, git seven white pebbles, and put dem in dish li'l cloth bag. When you want de axe ter cut, shake dem up."

Simon went off into the woods, and he started in to clear up the six acres. Then, remembering what Susanna had told him, he shook the red cloth bag. Right off, the axe flew out of his hands and began to chop the trees so fast that Simon only saw a cloud of wood chips.

Every time he shook the pebbles, the axe would cut, and the trees would fall, and the limbs would drop off, and the logs would roll up together, and the brush would pile itself up. He could have finished by the time the dinner horn blew, but he hung back, because he didn't want Susanna's daddy to know he'd done the work using conjurements. So he finished up the last bit himself. Two hours before sunset, the whole six acres was cleaned up.

Just then, the man came along with Susanna to see how the work was getting on—and was he ever surprised! He didn't know what to do or say. He wasn't about to give up his daughter to Simon. For a time he walked around and around and thought and thought about how he could get out of his bargain. At last, he said, "Look like you real forehanded wid yo' work."

Susanna smiled and put a finger to her lips. Simon shrugged and allowed, "Yasser: when I starts in on a job, I kayn't stop until I gits it done. Some er dis timber was rough an' tough, but I've had worser jobs dan dis in my time."

To himself, the witch wondered, What kind er folks is dis? Out loud he said, "Well, since yo' so spry, dey's two mo' acres 'cross de creek dar. Ef you clear dem up 'fo' supper, you kin come up ter de house and git de gal."

"Now, Papa, dat ain' fair!" protested Susanna. She was being careful not to let her daddy know that she wasn't the least bit worried on account of the magic she had given her sweetheart.

Meanwhile, Simon scratched his head because he wasn't sure if those pebbles would hold out. But Susanna gave him a wink, so he put on a bold face and told Susanna's father, "Well, sah, I'll go 'cross dere and clean up de two acres soon's I res' a bit."

45

The conjure man went on home, but Susanna lingered just long enough to rub her hair once more over the axe blade. Then she gave her beau a quick kiss and ran after her father. As soon as the others were out of sight, Simon jumped across the creek and shook the pebbles at the two acres of woods. Slick as owl grease, the trees were all cut down and piled up.

As soon as Susanna got home, her daddy said to her, "Daughter, it sure looks like Simon is gwine git you fo' his bride."

Clever Susanna just hung her head and looked fretful and said, "Oh, I don't care nuthin' special 'bout him." She was a sharp-eyed gal who saw just how angry her pa was getting because Simon had cleared the land. He could be a mighty mean witch, and she was afraid he might get suspicious if she seemed too happy about marrying Simon.

Well, when Simon come up to the house and said the two acres were cleared, the daddy made like he was glad for the way things turned out. But Susanna could see that he was really as sour as week-old buttermilk. When he went across to the barn, she took Simon by the hand and pulled him into the kitchen. She whispered, "Ef we don' run away dis ver' minute, Daddy's gwine kill you fo' sure!" Then she snatched a hen's egg out of a basket, a meal bag, and a skillet.

At first Simon said, "Oh, I cayn't believe what yo' tellin' me."

But Susanna just took him to the window and showed him where her daddy was coming across from the barn in the moonlight, carrying a big old knife and looking as angry as an old bull.

One see is worth twenty hears. Simon didn't argue when Susanna grabbed his hand and took off running. But he had a mighty hard time keeping up with the girl who ran as swiftly as a startled deer. Susanna didn't look back ever—just hauled Simon along with one hand, while she held the egg, meal bag, and skillet in her other.

When the witch man saw Simon and Susanna running away, he took right off after them, faster than lightning, with his knife in his hand. He was so mad, he snorted like a horse, while blue smoke came out of his nose and his eyes turned as red as a varmint's in the dark. He kept gaining on them, until, by'n'by, he had almost caught them. But Susanna yelled to Simon, "Fling down yo' coat."

The instant his coat touched the ground, a big thick wood sprang up. But the daddy, he just cut his way through it with his big, old knife and kept chasing after them.

Pretty quickly, he caught up to them again. But Susanna dropped the hen's egg on the ground; and when it broke, a big fog rose up out of the ground. For a time, the man got lost. But he conjured some fierce winds that blew the fog away, so he was chasing after the young folk again pretty quickly.

But when he got so close that he could almost grab Simon's shirttail, Susanna dropped the meal sack, and a big pond of water covered the ground where it fell. The man was in such a hurry that he first tried to drink it dry. When he found that he couldn't do this, he sat on the bank and blew on the water. His breath was hot as a furnace, and straight-away the water boiled off. Then he was after Simon and Susanna again.

As fast as the two lovers ran, the witch man ran faster. Having nothing left to try, Susanna dropped the skillet. Instantly a thick dark cloud fell down, and the man didn't know which way to go. But he had plenty of magic tricks of his own, and quickly, he made the darkness lift up, so that he could see where the others had gotten to. He made up for lost time, and pretty soon he was as close to them as the bark to the tree.

At this, Susanna said to Simon, "Take de red cloth bag I give you and drap a pebble."

Simon did this, and a high hill sprang up. But the witch climbed it lickety-split and kept on coming.

Then Susanna said, "Drap 'nother pebble."

This time, Simon dropped a bigger pebble, and a higher mountain popped up. But the man crawled up it and down it and came right on after the lovers.

Then Susanna said to Simon, "Fling down de whole bag."

The second he dropped it, a big rock wall rose up. It was so high that the witch man couldn't get over it. He ran up and down the length of it, snorting and shouting, but he couldn't find an end. Finally, after a long time, he gave up and went home.

On the other side of the high wall, Susanna sat down beside Simon, took his hand in hers, and said: "Now we kin rest."

And that's where their story ends.

# Women of the Midwest

# Sal Fink

## ANGLO AMERICAN

Sal Fink was the high-spirited, rambunctious daughter of Mike Fink, king of the flatboatmen. They sailed keelboats along the Mississippi, the Ohio, and the other great western rivers that were, for a time, America's most important highways. People could always spot Big Mike, often with Sal beside him, on their forty-foot craft named *The Light-Foot,* which was called a broadhorn because its steering oars angled like horns from two sides. They and their crew carried pioneer families and their possessions north and west or hauled freight to ports in the south. Mike or Sal would set the pace and the pole men, ranged on either side of the keelboat's passenger cabin, would strain to match them and keep the boat moving upstream or down.

Tall stories of Sal's deeds—like those of her father—were chronicled in newspapers, magazines, journals, and humorous writings. They thrilled American readers from the 1820s through the 1840s; today they provide a vivid look at life upon the great waterways before the arrival of the steamboat. So popular were the tales of Sal, Mike, and Sal's sharp-shooting mother, that they still turned up in print as late as the 1850s.

LEGENDARY MISSISSIPPI RIVER boatman Mike Fink had one daughter, Sal, who was a "ring-tailed roarer" in her own right. In fact, she became known far and wide as the "Mississippi Screamer," because of the way she would bellow *"Hi-i-i-i-i-ow-ow-ow-who-whooh!"* when she was feeling high-spirited or ready for a fight. Up and down the river she was known for fighting a duel with a thunderbolt, riding the river on the back of an alligator while "standen upright an' dancing 'Yankee Doodle,' " and even outracing a steamboat poling her own keelboat with a hand-picked crew.

The young woman was brave, hardy, and openhanded. She was dark-haired, handsome in a homespun way, short, and as sturdily built as her pa. Like him, she could be as kindhearted as a Connecticut grandmother or as rough as a Rocky Mountain bear.

Sal also took after her ma in grit as well as looks. She would tell how, one day before she was born, a thief broke into their cabin in the Kentucky wilderness. Her ma, doing the washing down by the creek, heard a noise and saw the thief running out of the cabin with a venison ham.

Mike was out hunting, so she picked up her gun and hunting knife (neither was very far from her side) and took off after the fellow. Finding that he could run faster than she, she took aim with her rifle and fired, winging the thief in his right thigh.

When the wounded man stumbled and fell, the woman whooped, "Gl—o—ree Hal—lay—*loo!*" Straightaway Mrs. Fink caught up with him, gathered up the stolen ham in her apron, and tied the villain's hands together. Then she dragged him back to the cabin.

"Jest you wait till Mike gets back," she said, as she went about fixing supper.

As it turned out, when Mike returned that evening, he took one look at the bruised and battered prisoner and said, "Seems t'me he's already suffered plenty." Then, to the thief, he said, "Give me your word you won't bother us agin, and you're a free man."

The fellow took one look at Mrs. Fink, who was sitting in a rocker cleaning her Kentucky rifle. He shuddered and said, "Lordy, you won't see *me* 'round these parts ever agin." Then he limped off as fast as his gimpy leg would allow.

And Sal was every bit as tough as her folks. One morning, when she was still a young child, she went out in the morning to gather acorns for her pigs. Hearing a curious sound from a huge hollow oak tree, she looked inside. With a terrible growl, a huge she-bear, followed by her cubs, took off after her. The old bear tried to grab her long hair or fringed buckskin skirt, while the young ones snapped at her heels with the fury of wildcats.

Turning, Sal gave a cry—*"Hi-i-i-i-i-ow-ow-ow-who-whooh!"*—that stopped all three bears in mid-snarl. Then she landed each of the cubs a tremendous kick—one that would have done a two-year-old colt proud—and sent them rolling over each other. But, before she could escape, the mother bear was upon her, trying to lock Sal in a deadly hug.

Using her naked fists, the young woman rained so many blows on the bear's chest that she soon knocked the wind out of the beast. But when she tried to escape from the reeling bear, she found the creature's teeth and claws so entangled in her hair that there was nothing more to do than pick up a piece of loose rock and deal the creature a death blow. "Sorry it come to that, old bar," she said, "but ma could double up a 'gator. I got my fambly honor to think 'bout—well's my own skin."

After this, she dragged the carcass home to show her father and mother. But when the cubs came sniffing around later, she took pity on them, fed them, and raised them as pets that would follow behind her like trained hounds.

One day in fall, Sal was out in the forest hunting wildcats to use their skins for the family's winter bedding. Suddenly, she found herself ambushed by a band of riverboat pirates. She was a regular tornado and put up a real "skrimmage," thumping heads and cracking some bones. But they had the numbers on her and the advantage of surprise. Soon they had her hog-tied. Then they carried her to Dead Man's Hollow, where the varmints tied her to a tree. Then they built a big bonfire, sat down around it in a circle, and set to arguing among themselves whether to kill the gal on the spot or hold her for ransom or sell her to the Indians—whatever would cause Mike Fink the most grief and give them the greatest satisfaction.

It turned out that they were the brothers of a river pirate named Cap'in Camilla. A few years before, Mike and his crew had tangled with the robbers who had a hideout near Cave-in-Rock, on the Ohio River. The battle was bloody, and things were touch and go for a while. But Mike's men got the upper hand and set fire to the outlaws' cabin. When the pirate chief and his daughter, Celia, tried to escape across the storm-ravaged river in a small boat, they foundered and both were drowned. Those pirates who did survive—mostly blood kin of Cap'in Camilla—vowed revenge on Mike one way or another. Ambushing Sal, they thought, was a stroke of luck.

As things turned out, they had another thought coming.

Sal bided her time, letting her eyes slide from the grim, dirty, un-shaven faces of the cutthroats to the pistols, knives, and daggers jammed in their broad belts. She thought that they were a pretty scruffy lot, with their filthy, red-and-black striped shirts, badly patched baggy trousers, and their beady eyes as bloodshot and red as the coarse red skullcaps they wore. "I swear," Sal said, testing the ropes that held her, "ever' one looks like he's been chawin' terbacker, an' spittin' ag'in the wind."

Anyhow, after much palavering and arguing and precious little decid-ing, the cutthroats pulled off their heavy boots and set their feet toward the blaze. "Lor'," said Sal, hitching as far back from the fire as she could, "it reminds me o' the time the skunks littered under th' barn!"

Soon the pirates began dropping off to sleep, one by one. By the time the bright moon was high in the sky, the last cutthroat was drifting off to sleep, snoring loudly enough to rouse the dead.

As soon as the last of the treacherous critters got to snoring, Sal, who had kept her temper in check, let her anger boil over. "I ain't agoin' t' stand any more sich treatment as this," she muttered. Then she burst all the ropes that held her as if they were no more than apron strings. After that, she stood with her hands on her hips studying the sleeping pirates and figuring out the best way to deal with them.

First, she disarmed them, stuffing the best pistols and daggers into her own belt and tossing the others into the brush. Then, spotting a pile of undamaged ropes, she tied the unconscious men's feet together all around the fire. Finally she wove a longer cord through the sleepers' bonds, holding the end in her hand.

"Wake, snakes!" she yelled, in a voice loud enough to set the woods trembling, "The fat's in the fire fur sartin!" With this, she gave a sudden, stupendous jerk that pulled all of them feetfirst into the fire, which was now mostly embers.

In an instant, the men were awake and yelling from fourteen pair of hotfeet. Sal, taking the wildcat pelts and a chest of gold—"In payment fur th' inconvennyence you sarpints caused me!" she cried—was off faster than a panther out of a pen. Behind her the burned men howled louder than one hundred tribes on the warpath. But Sal's triumphant bellow—*"Hi-i-i-i-i-ow-ow-ow-who-whooh!"*—drowned them out and sat honest folks bolt upright in their beds from the headwaters of the Ohio to the mouth of the Mississippi.

# Sweet Betsey from Pike

## ANGLO AMERICAN

*Oh, don't you remember sweet Betsey from Pike,*
*Who crossed the big mountains with her husband, Ike,*
*With two yoke of cattle, a large yellow dog,*
*A tall Shanghai rooster and one spotted hog.*

"Sweet Betsey from Pike" was one of the best-known songs that arose out of the gold rush to California in 1849 and immediately thereafter by those who hoped to strike it rich in that state. Robust, resourceful, courageous, with a sharp wit and an earthy laugh, Betsey embodies the women who risked all to reach the gold fields. Even more, she exemplifies the spirit of American pioneer women who helped tame the frontier.

The grueling trek carried Betsey and her husband Ike across Nebraska, Wyoming, Utah, Nevada, and on into California. The twists and turns of the California Trail took them through the Platte River Valley, over salt deserts, past the Great Salt Lake itself, and across the Sierras to California's mining regions.

Extremes of heat and cold, thirst and starvation—these were only some of the dangers faced by the gold seekers trudging west. Most feared was the threat of becoming "alkalied" by the mineral salts found in the water and arid soil of certain desert areas. Mark Twain, in *Roughing It*, described a stay in Nevada thus: "We camped two days in the neighborhood of the Sink of the Humboldt. We tried to use the strong, alkaline water of the Sink, but it . . . was like drinking lye, and not weak lye either. It left a taste in the mouth, bitter and every way execrable, and a burning in the stomach that was very uncomfortable." This is the final challenge that—almost—proves feisty Betsey's undoing.

BETSEY WAS A spunky gal, who had a sweet disposition and get-up-and-go enough for fifty. As ablaze with gold fever as her husband, Ike, she decided to risk everything on a bid to reach Calfornia and strike it rich in the goldfields there. So she and Ike sold their farm, loaded provisions into a covered wagon pulled by a team of oxen, and set out from Pike County, Missouri, along the California Trail.

One evening, in Nebraska, they pitched camp on the banks of the Platte River, where flat stretches of soft blue grass were made even bluer by plentiful lupine blossoms. The river, which had looked shallow, yellow, and muddy to Betsey earlier, now seemed streaked with gold by the setting sun.

"Y'know, Ike," Betsey said, dropping down on the grass when they'd pitched their tent under a stand of cottonwood trees and tended to the cattle and other animals, "it's okay here in Nebrasky, but I'm gonna be mighty glad to get to Californy and stake me a claim." She pulled off her boots and began rubbing her sore feet. "As it is, I feel I've been all over heck and half of Georgia since we left Pike County."

"Me, too," said Ike, who wasn't a man much given to words. He lay back on his elbows and chewed a blade of grass, listening to the sound of cicadas shrilling in the thin bushes.

At that moment the Shanghai rooster set up a terrible fuss.

"Lissen to that racketin'," Betsy said, "That critter oughtta have his tail feathers cut off right behind his ears. I'm sure he's too tough t'eat. Sometimes I wish he'd just run off."

"Me, too."

She got her wish the next day—and plenty of things she didn't wish for. One of the back wheels hit a rock, cracked, and came off their covered wagon, and down they went with a terrible crash. Cans of pork and beans, sacks of flour, their frying pan and coffeepot, tin plates and cutlery, a lantern, Betsey's trunk of clothes, and what-all spilled out of the back onto the prairie grass.

The oxen moaned, the yellow dog howled, the hog nosed through the spilled goods looking for food, and the old rooster lit out for the east.

"Must've chose to go back to Pike," said Betsey, as she helped Ike prop up the end of the wagon. "Good riddance t'bad roosters, I say."

But they had to stay where they were an extra day, while they repaired the broken wheel.

"I guess we was due for a bit o' bad luck," said Betsey. She was sitting beside Ike and watching the blue prairie that looked the same as the prairie she'd been watching for more days then she cared to think about.

"I guess," Ike agreed.


But this was only the start of their troubles. Before nightfall, the oxen had gotten into some poisonous jimson weed and died.

"Well, don't that beat all?" said Betsey, sitting on the bench of the wagon that clearly wasn't going any farther, unless she and Ike yoked themselves in and pulled it. She looked disgustedly at the canvas—once white as a ship's sail—that was now dingy with dust and torn by winds and storms. The wheels had blistered, the wagon sides were cracking, and the ironwork was rusting away in front of her eyes.

"Now what?" wondered Ike.

"We have us a beef roast tonight and cure the rest into jerky tomorrow. Can't let all that meat go t'waste," said Betsey. "'Sides, I always could think faster on a full stomach."

"Makes sense," said Ike.

So Betsey and Ike and the yellow dog had all the meat they could eat. And the hog dined happily off the scraps.

"Maybe things'll look better in the mornin'," said Betsey, crawling into the tent beside Ike.

"Hope so."

59

But things managed to look worse in the morning. No matter how they lightened the wagon, there was no way the two of them could get it moving. So Betsey sat down to fashion them rucksacks and carryalls from the canvas wagon cover. Meanwhile, Ike cured some of the beef over a fire to make jerky. The hardest of all was realizing how little they could carry and how much they would have to leave behind.

The next day, Betsey and Ike, the yellow dog and the spotted hog set out on foot. "Californy or bust," said Betsey, in a not very good mood. "We just busted. Now what?"

"Don't know," said Ike.

"Well, I hain't a-goin' back, so I guess I'm goin' ahead," Betsey said, putting the best face on things. "You with me?"

"Guess so."

On they went, broiling under the noonday sun and freezing at night because they'd left most of their blankets behind.

Pretty quickly, they finished off the last of their supplies, including the beef jerky. While they were considering whether to slaughter the spotted hog, the creature expired with a weary snort. "Mighty obligin' o'him t'save us s'much trouble," said Betsey, who was getting pretty angry at their run of bad luck, "but ol' porker here might be the luckiest o' all o' us."

"Might be," Ike agreed.

A few mornings later, Betsey sat frying the last piece of bacon over a fire of buffalo wood. Across from her, Ike sat looking mighty discouraged. Beside him, the dog drooped his tail and looked wondrously sad. Betsey divided up the last miserable bits of bacon, saving a taste for the dog, but nobody looked much happier for it.

"I swear, I'm still so hungry I could eat a sow and six pigs," Betsey admitted.

"Me, too," said Ike.

On they slogged, Betsey doing her best to cheer up Ike. At last, even the big yellow dog, shrunk to skin and bones, ran off to chase hares and never returned. This made Ike even more gloomy, so Betsey tried even harder to keep him going.

"We're bound t' reach Salt Lake City soon," said Betsey, looking at the tattered map she kept folded in her dress pocket.

"Hope so," said Ike.

Just when Betsey was feeling too weak and tired to take another step, they reached Salt Lake City. Things like flour and meat and beans came pretty dear, and the money they had with them didn't stretch very far. They had hoped to have enough to buy a mule to take with them on to California, but they had to settle for enough food and two new pairs of boots to get there under their own steam.

"I swear," said Betsey as they left Salt Lake City, "if I'd knowed what I know now, I'd o'took a ship and gone 'round the Horn to Californy. Couldn't take me no longer or cost me no more. Or mebbe I'd o' stayed back in Pike, and t' heck with Californy."

"Same here."

But the alkali desert west of Salt Lake was the worst stretch of all. The land was still and blisteringly hot under the scorching sun. All around them, the travelers could see broken wagons and the rib cages of oxen bleaching in the sun. "Ain't it awful?" Betsey complained. "I feel like hell ain't a mile away, 'n' all the fences are down."

"Yep," Ike agreed.

On and on the white and endless desert went. Grit flew into Betsey's eyes and mouth, so that she felt as blind as a noonday bat and as hoarse as a duck with a dumpling in its bill.

"I feel so unlucky," Betsey said at last. "It would be money in my pocket if I'd never been born."

Even being careful, they drained their canteens dry. They put bullets under their tongues just for a feeling of coolness. Time and again, Betsey would cry, "I see water over there!"

"Mirudge," Ike would say with a shrug.

At last, Betsey gave out. Distracted, she lay down in the sand and began rolling around in the sage and salt.

Ike, in surprise, dropped to his knees and cried, "Betsey, get up, you'll get sand in your eyes!"

At this, she sat up, and Ike saw tears, not sand, in the corners of her eyes. "Oh, Ike, let's go back to Pike County again. Otherwise, it won't be long till you'll be puttin' pennies on m'eyes and pullin' a blanket over m'face."

"Sweet Betsey, my darling," said Ike, and gave her a hug. "You can't give up now! Where's my gal who could put out hell with one bucket o'water?" Then he whispered in her ear, "My sweet Pike County rose," his nickname for her when he had come courting.

It might have been the shock of Ike coming on so talkative and affectionate that acted like smelling salts for Betsey. More likely, it was her own stubborn refusal to give up the fight, since she had always had spunk and to spare. In any case, Betsey tapped a wellspring of courage inside. She stood up, wiped the last of the gritty tears from her eyes, and shouted, "Californy or bust!"

Ike put his arm around her waist.

"Let's go!" he said.

Not long after this, they spotted Pilot Peak, the great purple mound that could be seen everywhere, from Idaho, Nevada, and Utah. There they found green bulrushes and salt grass guarding clear, cool pools of water.

Refreshed, they forged on from Carson Sink, through Hope Valley, over Carson Pass, past Spring Lake, Silver Springs, and Tragedy Flat. Arm in arm they went, until they reached California. Late one evening, they stood on a very high hill, looking down on Placerville, their goal. Ike and Betsey sighed contendedly, then started down the hill into town.

As it turned out there was a dance at the town hall that same night. Ike slapped the dust out of his striped Pike County pants, while Betsey put a ribbon in her hair and some rings on her fingers.

While a fiddler scraped out a tune, many a miner came up and asked Betsey to dance. "I will, ol' hoss," she would agree, then add, "But don't dance me too hard: my feet are still tender and my head's full of dust!"

But Ike became jealous. So he started flirting with a woman who was painted like a new saloon. Pretty soon Betsey noticed Ike with his arm around the woman's waist. She stormed over and said, "You got a grin on you like a jackass eating briars."

Well, that set Ike off. For the second time in less than a month, the two of them had a real exchange of words—only this time, they were haranguing each other with the passion and volume of a pair of stump orators. When the disagreement got so loud that no one could hear the fiddler, Ike and Betsey were tossed out into the street.

Finally, Ike said, "That's it, I'm through. Livin' with you has always been as easy as shinnyin' up a thorn tree with an armload o' eels." And he marched off down the street.

"Good-bye, you big lummox," Sweet Betsey shouted after him. "I'm glad you've backed out!"

"Me, too!" he yelled back.

"Well," said Betsey, plunging her head several times into a horse trough to clear it, "I've got from Pike t' Placerville in one piece. Who knows what's gonna happen next?" Then, cupping her hands around her mouth, she shouted after the disappearing Ike, "Might could be, we'll even get us back t'gether. And if not," she assured herself, squeezing the water out of her hair, "I ain't the loser, no matter how the cards is cut."

Even though the ballad "Sweet Betsey from Pike" ends with each going in a different direction, it seems likely that Ike and Betsey—a team who crossed rivers, prairie, desert, and mountains; faced sunstroke, starvation, seasonal and unseasonal weather—got back together sooner or later. It's just that nobody got around to telling that part of their story. So now I have.

# Old Sally Cato

## AFRICAN AMERICAN

This story, recorded in Missouri, has numerous African anteced-
ents, to which I have added details. Many of these African stories
involve a flesh-eating elephant that swallows people whole, until
an old woman, with knife and digging stick, lets herself be swallowed up. She then finishes off the elephant from within. Afterward, she cuts a way for all those inside the elephant to gain their
freedom.

Folklorist Roger D. Abrahams, commenting on a version
from Guyana titled "Crawling into the Elephant's Belly," notes
that, "This strange and gory story is widely reported in the New
World. . . . It invokes one of the most common of all Afro-
American episodes, in which a prohibition against eating too
much results in the capture and/or death of the Trickster [and]
often occurs inside a large animal's body."

Whatever its origins, "Old Sally Cato" is a story of pure fun.

---

ONE MORNING IN autumn Old Sally Cato, a widow woman, rose with the
chickens in her cabin far back in the Missouri hill country. She set out
biscuits and gravy and hot coffee, then rousted her two sons, Big Tom
and Li'l Jack, out of bed by lifting the bedsteads and spilling the two onto
the floor.

"Time fer you t' go 'n' fetch one o' the cattle," she said. "You bring
it on back, kill it, skin it, and git the beef ready so's I can cure it. I want
t' be sure we have plenty o' meat for the winter."

Li'l Jack, who had a small voice, whined, "Couldn't we wait'll next week or so? Thass a lot o' work."

"It'll be the same amount o' work next week or next month," said his ma, "but *winter* won't hold back, even if *you* do. Now go." Then she said, "And be careful you don't do anything to rouse Billy Bally Bully."

At the name of the giant who lived beyond the hill, both Li'l Jack and Big Tom began to shake. They knew that the horrible monster—as big as a mountain or bigger—was an old greedy gut who'd as soon swallow a man as look at him.

"Maybe we *should* wait a mite afore fetchin' that beef," said Tom.

"Git!" said their mother, and they got.

Sally dragged her old spinning wheel onto the porch, shaded by bittersweet vines. Watching her two sons going off drag-foot toward the pasture where the cattle were kept, she sighed and shook her head. "I swear, if their brains was in birds' heads, all the birds o' the air would fly backwards."

Then she set to her spinning. *"Squeakity-whirr-whirr-whirr,"* went the old spinning wheel. *"Squeakity-whirr-whirr-whirr."*

Meanwhile, Jack and Tom trudged toward the high pasture. Along the way, they were startled by a sudden fluttering of crows from a nearby meadow. The birds shot up to the sky like a cloud of black smoke.

"Well," said Li'l Jack, "them crows mean bad luck."

"Oh," said Big Tom, "you listen to Ma too much. A crow don't mean nothin' more'n a crow."

But when they got to the pasture where the beef cattle should have been grazing, they found it empty. The little herd had wandered even farther back among the hills.

"Now what?" grumbled Tom in his booming voice.

But Jack dropped to his knees and searched among the grasses and fallen leaves, until he found a grandaddy long-legs. Holding the insect gently in the palm of his hand, he asked:

Grandaddy long-legs, where are the cows?
Grandaddy long-legs, where are the cows?

As he watched closely, the insect lifted one slender leg and pointed to the west. "That way," said Jack confidently, letting the spider go back to its leaf pile.

"I swear, you 'n' Ma are two of a kind," said Tom. But he followed his brother higher into the hills where the butternuts and hickory and elm grew thickest.

The higher they climbed, the more they kept eyes and ears peeled for any sign of Billy Bally Bully. They were dangerously close to the giant's territory, and they knew that anyone the monster caught trespassing would be gobbled up faster than a duck swallows a June bug.

At last, they found the missing cattle in a tiny meadow that neither of them had seen before. Straightaway, Big Tom selected the fattest animal and knocked it over the head with his hammer.

"Why'd you do that?" asked Jack.

"So's we can do our work here without Ma watchin' and sayin' as how we're doin' it all wrong and makin' us take twice the time to git done," answered Tom. "Now help me hang this carcass from the tree so's we can skin it and dress it."

"But, Ma said—" Jack began.

"You just pipe down 'n' start skinnin'," his brother said.

They worked for a little while. Then Jack stopped suddenly and said, "I hear somethin'."

"No you don't," said his brother. "Keep workin'."

Jack worked a bit longer, then said, "I hear somethin', only it's nearer."

"No you don't." Tom didn't look up from his work. "Keep workin'."

Suddenly they both stopped, because this time both of them had heard a *"BOOM! BOOM!"* like thunder over the hill. A minute later, they saw Billy Bally Bully tromping over the hill with no more effort than a widow climbing a stile to cross a fence.

To the frightened brothers, the giant looked bigger than the mountain itself. His black hair stood up like a grove of trees, his eyes were as big around as wagon wheels, and his mouth (filled with yellow teeth the size of tombstones) looked wide enough to swallow half the county. The giant sniffed the air with nostrils as big and black and deep as the pits of hell.

The frightened boys hugged each other and shook, too scared to move.

*"I SMELL FRESH MEAT. WHAT YOU DOIN'?"* asked the giant.

"Skinnin' beef," said Tom, his voice suddenly as small as Jack's.

*"GIVE ME SOME."*

Quick as a wink, Tom cut a big chunk of meat and tossed it to the giant, who gulped it down whole.

The giant licked his lips. *"GIVE ME MORE,"* he demanded.

Tom sliced off an even bigger slab and threw it into the monster's outstretched palm.

The giant swallowed it right down. *"MORE!"* he roared.

Soon Jack and Tom were cutting up the beef carcass as fast as they could and flinging it at Billy Bally Bully. But every helping only made the giant hungrier.

*"MORE!"* he thundered. *"MORE! MORE! MORE!"*

"There ain't no more," said Jack, whose voice had shrunk to a whisper.

*"THEN I'LL EAT YOU!"* rumbled the giant, stretching out a hand as big as a barn.

But before he could grab the brothers, they took off running like sixty for home. Behind them, they heard the *BOOM! BOOM! BOOM!* of the giant following them. On every side, the trees danced up and down with each deafening *BOOM!*

Fear put wings on the brothers' feet. In next to no time, they had reached the little cabin where their mother sat working her spinning wheel, *Squeakity-whirr-whirr-whirr.*

"Ma, Ma!" they screeched, "Billy Bally Bully's after us!"

"What did you do to rile him up?" asked Old Sally, suspiciously. Now she could hear the *BOOM! BOOM!* of the onrushing giant.

"Nothin'," said Jack. "We was just skinnin' the beef—"

"You did your skinnin' back in the hills?" she exclaimed. "Ain't I tol' you time and agin that there's nothin' like the smell o' fresh meat t' bring Billy Bally Bully sniffin' around?"

*BOOM!*

"He's gonna eat us, Ma!" wailed Tom.

*BOOM! BOOM!*

"And I'm of half a mind to let him," she said. "You two are as sorry as a pair of worn-out shoes."

Now the shingles of the cabin roof and the ground shook from the *BOOM! BOOM! BOOM!* of the giant's tread. The woman's hound dog, Blue, howled *"Owooooo!"* from under the porch. A second later, the animal was off and running.

"Hide us, Ma!" Tom and Jack yelled. They were so frightened, their teeth were rattling as loud as hogs eating charcoal.

Sally pointed to the big old kettle in the yard that she used for making soap. "Upend that pot 'n' hide yourselves under it. I'll see to old greedy guts myself."

Just before Billy Bally Bully lumbered into view, Old Sally Cato had returned to her spinning. Under her apron she had tucked a feather duster, a pair of knitting needles, and a carving knife. Looking up at the gangling, hairy-faced creature glaring down at her, Sally had to keep a tight hold on her courage as well as her feet, which wanted to hightail it across hedgerows and cornfields as fast as her hound dog had.

*"WHAR'D THEM FELLAS GO?"* the giant asked. He sniffed the air. *"THEY'S AROUND. I SMELL 'EM."*

The old woman pretended to pay him no mind. Her spinning wheel went *Squeakity-whirr-whirr-whirr.*

In a voice so loud that it rattled the roof over her head, Billy Bally Bully demanded, *"WHAR THEY HIDIN'?"*

Still the old woman gave all her attention to the spinning wheel, *Squeakity-whirr-whirr-whirr.*

*"YOU DEEF, OL' WOMAN?"* The giant got down on his hands and knees and pushed his bristly face close to the woman's. He opened his mouth wide to shout in her ear.

At that instant, Old Sally ran into his mouth, all the way to the back. Then she shook the feather duster about, releasing great clouds of dust that made the giant wheeze and sneeze. The old woman hung onto his tonsils for the worst of this, then she slid down his gullet into his stomach.

There she ran around, jabbing at his insides with her knitting needles, giving Billy Bally Bully the granddaddy of all gut aches. The pain was so fearful that the monster bellowed and stamped and ran around in circles, knocking down one corner of the porch and smashing the wheelbarrow flat. Tom and Jack peeped out from under the soap kettle and saw Billy Bally Bully frantically waving his arms like a windmill gone to the bad and sounding like a dying calf in a hailstorm. The whole countryside shook as if hit by an earthquake.

Inside the giant, the old woman found his heart. Then she took her carving knife and finished him off, lickety-split. But, even though dead, Billy Bally Bully was too dumb to fall over. For a long time, he just stood glassy-eyed, while the brothers, under the soap kettle, tried to guess what had happened.

Suddenly, the giant pitched over backward like a felled tree. The force of him hitting the ground raised the cabin and barn and outhouse ten feet in the air, before they dropped back into place.

Matter-of-factly, the old woman cut herself free of the giant. Then she called to her two sons and showed them the beef lying unharmed inside the giant, who had swallowed each chunk whole. None of it was a bit harmed.

"Now then," said the woman, "carry that beef out t' the smoke-house—it'll be dusk-dark soon. And next time, when I tell you t' do something' or not t' do somethin', you lissen good."

"Yes, ma'am," Big Tom and Li'l Jack answered.

"Good," said Old Sally. "Now you git on with your bizness, 'n' let me git on about mine.

"I swear, these days it ain't nothin' but one inneruption after t' other," she said. In no time, though, she was happily humming to herself while her spinning wheel went *Squeakity-whirr-whirr-whirr.*

# Women of the Southwest

# Pale-Faced Lightning

## PUEBLO

In the American West the region around Mount Superstition (not far from Phoenix) has long had a reputation as the source of many legends and has also been the object of many fears. The mountain is crowned with eroded forms resembling human figures: these have given the mountain its name. A Pima Indian legend says that these shapes were once Indians who sought refuge on the mountaintop from a great flood. They were warned not to make a sound until all the waters had dried up, but they disobeyed. In punishment, the gods turned them into stone. Superstition Mountain is also reportedly the site of the famous Lost Dutchman Mine, the subject of countless tales. Accounts of its hidden riches have led dozens of searchers to their deaths in futile attempts to discover its whereabouts.

This part of Arizona is home to several Pueblo tribes, including Hopi and Zuni. *Pueblo* is a Spanish word meaning "town" and is used to designate those Native Americans who lived in such villages or cities—some still inhabited, some whose ruins are scattered across New Mexico and Arizona. Although the people of different pueblos had their own languages, their manner of life and thought was very similar.

Although the mysterious tribe that Pale-Faced Lightning ruled over is not named in legend, I have given them some of the customs of the Hopis, because details of the story suggest similarities to that people's way of life. The identity of the mysterious fair-haired woman remains the most intriguing part of the legend.

Was she part of some early expedition from beyond the sea?

Ancient records have suggested that America was visited by the Greeks, Romans, Vikings, Chinese, Japanese, Egyptians, Phonenicians, Hebrews, Arabs, and Turks—often long before Columbus. Perhaps Pale-Faced Lightning's story is linked to the mystery of the Mandans, Native Americans who lived along the Missouri River. They often had blue eyes and hair that turned white in old age—traits that no other Native Americans have shown. Many think that they intermarried with Welsh explorers who may have landed in what is now Alabama in 1170. The tribe was wiped out by smallpox in the mid-1800s, before the truth could be discovered. Might Pale-Faced Lightning have been a Mandan? The truth is forever lost in the past, where the historical event became legend.

HUNDREDS OF YEARS ago, a tribe of little people—the tallest barely above three feet—moved into the area around Mount Superstition. Amid the waste of sagebrush and rabbit bush, they built themselves a pueblo atop a mesa. In front of the settlement was a huge pool of water that supplied the needs of the village.

Next they planted fields of maize, pumpkins, beans, squash, and cotton. They dug ditches to bring water from distant creeks for the plants and vines. They also raised herds of sheep and flocks of turkeys, which they considered more important for feathers that they could use for decoration than for eating.

In the center of their fields, they raised a lookout post—a wooden platform two stories high with a brush roof. From here a guard watched for birds or small animals that threatened the fields—or for Apache raiders.

They were a peaceful people, resourceful yet strong, although the tallest brave among them stood less than four feet. They often managed to keep their superstitious enemies at bay with their ceremonies and chanting in honor of the sun. The rumble of their tall drums of cottonwood and hide, the ghostly sound of bells, and the words of their ancient songs were more impressive than a show of arms. Hearing this, Apaches or Comanches would skirt their fields to prey on other, less-fearsome settlements.

Then, one day at noontime, the guard in his watchtower began to beat his warning drum. He had spotted a solitary human figure running toward the fields from the south. On every side the men, who did the farming and herding (as well as the hunting), looked up from their work amid the rows of corn and squash. Carrying spears or simply digging sticks, these farmers rushed to drive the invader from their fields.

To their astonishment, they discovered a woman, nearly collapsing from heat and weariness, staggering toward them. She was dressed in a white cotton dress and shawl decorated with designs from the Zuni people far to the south. But what caused the men to gape in wonder was the woman's white face, fair hair, and height—she was half again as tall as the tallest man among them.

She spoke to them in halting words of the Zuni tongue. Her words were curiously accented, but a few among the people were able to understand her well enough. One who did was Lololomai, the old man who was spokesman for his people.

"I have run away from those people who live over there," she explained, pointing to the south where the Zuni people lived. "I was a stranger among them, and lived in peace with them for a time. But I would not marry the man they said I must. I have heard that you are a civilized people who welcome strangers if they mean you no harm. I ask you to let me stay for a time with you. In return, I will work to earn my food and teach you some of the ways of my people."

"You are not Zuni," said Lololomai. "Who are your people?"

"My people live in a place far to the east, beyond the mountains that the sun must climb each dawn." Then she spoke the name of her people and the name of the place where they lived. But the sounds were strange—impossible for the small people to understand.

Lololomai said, "We greet you as a friend. We will not turn you away if you wish to stay. We will not make you stay if you choose to leave."

"You are a generous people," she said.

"We are a civilized people," the old man said with a shrug. "No more."

So the woman was assigned duties to perform. She helped the women tend the small gardens near the pueblo and make *piki,* thin sheets of cornmeal breadstuff baked on red-hot rock slabs. She helped the men who did the weaving, spinning, moccasin making, and fuel gathering. In return, she was given a space to live in and a share of the community's food. Though she had come from another place, she was respected, as were all women. They owned the houses, food, seed for the next year's plantings, and the springs and pools around the pueblo, including the vast, deep pool in front of the village.

For her part, the stranger taught the small people new methods of weaving and curing meats and healing sickness or wounds. Because of her wisdom and skills, she was soon welcomed at the "Chiefs' Talk"— the meeting of village elders and heads of various groups that was held each winter. Her advice, delivered in soft, strangely accented, carefully measured words, was always listened to and acted upon. With her help, the people found that their crops were more bountiful, their children were healthier, and the Apache raids had grown less frequent as the woman taught them new ways to protect their homes and fields.

Sometimes, however, the people would see her standing on the highest roof of the pueblo, her eyes fixed on some point far to the east. At first they did not understand, but they soon realized that she was looking toward the rising sun because that was where her true home was. More and more, their fear grew that she would abandon them one day and try to return to that place from whence she had come.

Finally, the day came that they dreaded. "Though it causes my heart to break, I soon must leave you," she said. "I long to visit my people again, who live there, beyond the eastern mountains."

They begged her not to go away; and old Lololomai, with tears in his eyes, reminded her how much the people loved her and how important she had become to the life of the pueblo. But when he saw that her heart was set on leaving them, he said simply, "If we kept you when you have chosen to go, we would not be civilized people. Go where you must go, but keep us always in your heart."

She said nothing—just smiled a sad smile and touched her hand to her heart to show that wherever she journeyed, a part of them would travel with her.

But on the dawn of the day when she was to depart, word reached the pueblo that a huge war party of Zunis was advancing from the south. The small people were terrified that the enemy would lay waste to their fields and destroy their village.

There had been an uneasy truce between the two peoples for a while. For a long time the Zunis had insisted that the small people had claimed lands that properly belonged to them.

Cries of alarm swept the pueblo. Clearly this was no mere raiding party to be driven off with singing and drumming, or with arrows and digging sticks. This was a Zuni war band that marched confidently; the warriors were sure that their own medicine would protect them. In their distress, the small people turned to the pale woman whose wisdom had provided them with such powerful medicine before.

"Why do they make war on us now?" asked Lololomai.

"Who can say?" the woman responded. "I lived among them long enough to know that they are a people quick to take the warpath if they feel they have been wronged."

"What can we do against an enemy who is so strong?" asked Lololomai.

"We are a civilized people," said the woman. For a moment she hesitated, glancing at the water jug and food that she had set out for her journey home; then she smiled grimly at Lololomai. "Let us go out to meet the invaders. Perhaps talk will send them home. But let us also be a wise people and do what we can to defend our pueblo."

She instructed those who remained behind to hide the sheep and turkeys in secret valleys; to carry all provisions, tools, and weapons from the fields below up to the mesa top; and to place piles of stones along the edge of the cliffs above the path that wound up to the pueblo. Then she marched out with a party of warriors and elders to meet the Zunis.

It was agreed by all that Lololomai would speak for the mesa dwellers. Though it left a bitter taste in her mouth, the pale-faced woman had suggested this, because she knew the Zunis would be more respectful of a man.

But when they faced the enemy across a small streambed, they were dismayed to find that the Zuni chief immediately recognized the pale-faced woman and arrogantly demanded, "You must hand her over to me at once. She is the cause of all this trouble. We have a claim upon her. My people brought her many moons ago from the waters of the rising sun. It was only to escape an honorable marriage with me that she fled to you small people."

"A civilized people would not make a slave of such a person," Lololomai objected.

"Our ways are not your ways," said the Zuni chief. "If you do not return the white-faced one to us, we will take her by force. Give her to us, and we will leave you in peace."

Then the woman, who had remained silent until now, said, "If you hand me over to them, they will still attack our pueblo. All the time I was with them, they talked of killing, so that they could have our fields and goods and homes."

"We will not give her to you," said the spokesman to the Zuni chief.

"Then we will take her by force," said the chief, "and we will kill you and take everything you own, because you have not surrendered her to us."

At this, the woman and the small people hurried back to their home. Behind them, the Zunis, who had been slowed by the swift current and slippery mud of the stream, howled and beat their war drums and made ready to attack the pueblo.

Then the enemy, some seven hundred strong, marched on the pueblo. The small people had set up several ambushes and dug pits, but they gathered their real forces to defend their pueblo. With such limited resistance, the Zuni warriors soon reached the base of the mesa. When they tried to climb toward the top, the people rained rocks and arrows on them. But despite the small people's best efforts, the Zunis made their way to the top.

As the enemy warriors massed at the trailhead, the mesa dwellers gathered in a half circle behind the pale woman. She stood across the great pool of water, calm and commanding, her white robe and light brown hair fluttering in the wind. Both friend and foe looked upon her with admiration.

Then, with a cry, the Zunis rushed toward her, brandishing clubs and spears. Before they could reach her, the pale-faced woman stooped, picked up an earthen jar, and emptied its contents into the pool. In an instant she ran back, crying a warning to her people, "Run away! Do not look back!"

Hissing sparks and blazing balls of fire leaped from the surface of the pool, while tongues of silver-white flame burst from fissures in the ground. When these unearthly fires touched the Zunis, they fell dead. Others, fearful of this mysterious fire or blinded by it, plunged over the edge of the cliff to their deaths. The small people surged forward and drove the survivors back. That was the only effort needed to urge the remainder of the war party to full retreat.

"How have you done this thing?" asked the old Lololomai, when the dust of battle had settled. "If we could do this, we would not be afraid when you leave us. Can you teach us how to do this for ourselves?"

"I cannot teach the secret to you," the woman answered. "This is something only my people can do. But I have decided that I cannot leave you. You are my people now. My home is among you."

"That is a very good thing," said the old man. "I am grateful for this, though I know this must put pain in your heart."

Many months later, a band of Apaches, under a new war chief, attempted to raid the pueblo. They fell upon the people with suddenness and ferocity. Before the alarm could be sounded, many of the farmers were killed. Once again, the woman the mesa dwellers called the "Pale-Faced Lightning" repelled the attackers by creating her deadly fire. This time, the slaughter was even greater.

A second time, the woman looked on the scene of many deaths. Finally, she said, "More enemies will come soon. This is no longer a good place for a civilized people. It is time for us to make another place our home."

Before the next full moon, the small people left as suddenly as they had come. The Apaches who claimed their deserted fields and pueblos said that the strange people had gone to live in a secret cavern in the mountains, where the Pale-Faced Lightning still rules them.

Other Apaches have held that her spirit haunts a cave on Superstition Mountain itself, where her body one day vanished in a blaze of fire.

Others of the same tribe have pointed out a second cave, on the south side of Salt River, as the place where the woman's spirit dwells. Still others claim that a skeleton and robes of a strange, silky texture, beautifully ornamented, were once found there.

More recent visitors—those who disbelieve such old tales of wonder—note that electrical phenomena are common on the mountain. They suggest that iron, copper, and other deposits lying close together may account for the ghostly fires sometimes glimpsed in the caves or on the mountainside.

But those who believe her story know that Mount Superstition is her home, and they cherish the legend of the Pale-Faced Lightning.

# Pohaha

## TEWA

The Tewa live in the area of Santa Fe, New Mexico. They are primarily an agricultural people, raising corn, vegetables, and fruits in the desert region—always struggling against drought and sandstorms. Like other Pueblo peoples, they are skilled potters, weavers, basket makers, and builders. The Spanish conquistadores who first contacted pueblo dwellers called them the "finest" people they encountered—noble of bearing and handsome of feature.

The Pueblo peoples spoke many different languages, and each village existed as an independent political grouping; but the people recognized a common ancestry, traded with other pueblos, sometimes intermarried, and shared many similar values, religious beliefs, and world views. They held that people must live in harmony with nature, and out of this grew a rich cultural tradition expressed in legends, poetry, songs, dance, and art. The heart of each pueblo was the *kiva*, a special underground chamber with a rounded roof extending aboveground. The entrance was a hole in the center of the roof, through which a ladder reached to the the pounded-earth flooring below. Here private prayers were offered and group ceremonies performed throughout the year to ask for blessings, assure bountiful crops, and give thanks for good health.

Although it was unusual, it was not unheard of for women to become warriors in their own right, as does Pohaha in the story that follows. Stories of warrior women are well known among many tribes: Lozen was an Apache warrior-maid; Chief Earth Woman led the Ojibwa on the warpath; Ehyophsta (Yellow-

Haired Woman) was a Cheyenne who distinguished herself in combat; and like Pohaha, a young woman, He-e-e, of the Hopi—another Pueblo people—helped saved her village from a raiding party.

AMONG THE TEWA people, who live in adobe pueblos along the Rio Grande, there was once a girl, Pohaha. She had such a quick temper and was so strong-willed that day after day she refused to obey her mother or father. Soon they tired of telling her what to do and just let her be.

At dances, when women were expected to behave much more politely and quietly than men, this young woman would often raise her knees as high as men did, or hop back and forth with yells as loud as her male partners. She would not sing as women sang—in a thin voice—but would belt out a song in a loud and full-throated manner that did not make her many friends.

She was not content to engage in such activities as gathering willows and reeds to weave into baskets or shaping clay into pots to be dried by the sun—things that were the work of women. Instead, Pohaha made herself a bow and arrow and a throwing stick to hunt rabbits and added a great amount of game to the family's stores. But although they ate the meat willingly enough, no one could accept Pohaha's persistent refusal to behave as her mother, aunts, and the other women of the pueblo did.

Even though she became impatient with her elders and the rigid ways of her people, she never grew weary of the land. Day after day, she would happily lose herself among the restless patterns of light and shadow that the sun and clouds cast over mountains and valleys and mesas. At certain times of the year, near evening, sun and rain would create a rainbow, *kwantembe,* that arched across earth and sky—so beautiful that Pohaha's heart would catch in her throat. Often she would sit by the entrance to her family's apartment at night to watch *Posendo,* the moon, make his way from east to west. At all such moments, she would sing a song to Nanechukwiyo, the Earth Mother, for the beauty of her realm.

But, despite the power of the world around her, Pohaha could never feel at ease. She knew too well that her people lived in constant fear. While some men tended the fields of corn, beans, and squash near the pueblo, other men, women, and children kept watch for the appearance of raiding parties from other tribes that were a constant threat.

One day, while Pohaha was grinding corn, a Comanche raiding party drew near the village. Her uncle came and grabbed her arm and said to her, "You who would not mind us, choosing to behave like a boy: Take your bow and arrows and go and fight the enemies who are coming. This is your chance to go and prove yourself as brave as a man would be."

"Ha!" cried the girl. "I am eager to go and fight our enemies. I am not afraid. I will show them that my courage is as great as any warrior's!"

She accepted the bow and arrows that her uncle held out to her. From the wall in the corn-grinding room, she took a gourd rattle that only male dancers had used before. Shaking this, she sang a war song of her own composing four times as she danced inside the room.

> Behold, the fierce woman, she am I!
> The fierce woman!
>
> Bow of mulberry wood have I.
> Behold, the fierce woman, she am I!
> The fierce woman!
>
> Arrows tipped with flint have I.
> Behold, the fierce woman, she am I!
> The fierce woman!
>
> My heart is strong as flint inside me,
> Living strong—my heart of flint.

89

Behold, the fierce woman, she am I!
The fierce woman!

I strike my enemy and return.
Like zigzag lightning I strike my foe,
Returning singing a victory song.
Behold, the fierce woman, she am I!
The fierce woman!

Then she took a mask down from the wall. One side was painted blue and one side was yellow, and it had long teeth.

Wearing this, she went outside and danced in the plaza, singing her war song again four times. Whenever she paused in her singing, Pohaha cried, "Ha! Ha!" she was so eager to fight. So she challenged the men to match her warlike spirit.

At last, putting aside the mask and ignoring the sneers of her people, she grabbed a spear and a shield woven like a basket. Throwing aside her cotton shawl and tying her bow and arrows across her back, Pohaha charged forth to meet the Comanche raiders who had reached the edge of the farthest cornfield.

The fighting was fierce, but the Tewa beat back attack after attack. The girl herself killed two of the enemy with her arrows, and a third with her spear. In the heat of battle, many of the warriors were inspired by Pohaha's selfless courage. Soon after this, the remainder of the raiding party broke and ran.

"Ha! Ha!" cried the young woman, and the men beside her took up her cry as their victory chant. Pohaha led the warriors back to the village, singing and laughing. When the people gathered in the plaza the next morning to dance in celebration of their victory, she carried a flat gourd rattle and a tiny bow and arrow just as the men did. All the Tewa people were very respectful of the young woman warrior.

That night, her uncles came to her mother's house and told Pohaha,

"It is our wish that you become our *ahkonutuyo*, war chief. Though you are not a man, you are the bravest one among us."

Pohaha nodded solemnly, saying, "I accept this great honor you give me, and the burden of duty you place upon me." As war chief, she would have to lead her people against enemies, protect them from sickness, and treat them as her children.

Year after year, she kept the pueblo's defenses always ready to meet a fresh attack from Comanche, Pawnee, Apache, or Kiowa raiders. She led the Tewa on raiding parties to keep their enemies on the defensive. She laid out the plans for battle when full-size war parties threatened her people. No matter how terrible the fighting, the woman's triumphant cry, "Ha! Ha!" was always heard at battle's end.

She became an important part of her people's lives. One of her most important duties was to select the men and women to dance the all-important roles of Corn Maidens, the Buffalo Mothers, and the Buffalo Fathers in the dances that were the heart of Pueblo life.

She changed her womanly clothes for a man's cotton kilt, a robe of rabbit fur and turkey feathers, and a braided cotton sash. Wearing her mask, she would set the ferocious pace of the war dance.

Even when she grew too old to hunt or fight, the newly chosen war chiefs went to her for advice and encouragement. Children would listen enthralled while she recounted the stories of her life. She reminded them to love and care for the land that Nanechukwiyo had given them, and to do whatever was demanded of them to protect it.

"My spirit will be with you all the time," Pohaha promised when she died. "The mask is me," she said, giving her blue and yellow mask to her people.

For many years after that, the people kept the mask in the pueblo's kiva and honored it. It was the mask of their great warrior hero.

# Sister Fox
# and Brother Coyote

## MEXICAN AMERICAN

Tales of resourceful Sister Fox (Hermana Zorra) and her stronger, but far less sensible cousin, Brother Coyote (Hermano Coyote), are widely known throughout the American Southwest.

Sister Fox, who is *muy ladina* (very sly), is a cousin of Br'er Rabbit, a classic trickster figure; her encounter with the wax figure parallels Br'er Rabbit's meeting with the tar baby in Joel Chandler Harris's Uncle Remus Stories. Like the contraction *Br'er* for "Brother," the names of Hermana Zorra and Hermano Coyote are sometimes shortened to 'Mana Zorra and 'Mano Coyote.

IN THE DESERT country of the Southwest, there was once a very clever fox. She had been stealing a chicken every night from a certain *ranchero,* Don Perez. After having failed many times to trap the sly vixen, the man finally hit upon the idea of creating a manlike figure of soft, sticky wax to guard his henhouse and capture her.

When Sister Fox saw the little figure sitting in the moonlight outside the henhouse, she paused to size up the stranger. Always cautious, she watched for a long time, finally deciding that the small creature, looking so pale and still, posed no threat to her. Boldly she approached the mannikin and said, *"¡Buenas noches, amigo!"*

Of course, the little wax figure did not answer back. Several times the fox spoke to him, and always the insufferable person ignored her pleasantries. At last, angered by so much rudeness, Sister Fox grabbed him with her paws. She intended to shake some manners into him. Instead, she found herself stuck fast. The more she struggled to free herself, the more firmly she found her paws and fur wed to the sticky wax.

At that moment, Brother Coyote, who also had a hunger for the *ranchero's* chickens, came by.

"*¡Hola, amiga!*" called the coyote, "*¿Qué tal?*"

Now the fox and coyote were cousins, but they were also rivals. They often found themselves after the same prize, and each such meeting became a contest between them. Sometimes Brother Coyote won, because he was bigger and stronger. But more often Sister Fox won, because she was clever and knew that brains could often get the better of brawn.

"Hello, dear cousin," replied Sister Fox in her most honeyed voice. "You have come just in time to help me. If you do this, you will also help yourself to a nice, fat chicken." She knew only too well that the coyote would more likely help her because of hunger in his belly rather than goodness in his heart.

Licking his chops at the thought of a tasty hen, Brother Coyote asked his cousin, "Please, explain yourself."

"Oh," said the wily fox, "Don Perez has agreed to let me have one chicken each night. This is to thank me for a certain small favor I did him."

"And what favor is that?" asked the coyote.

"A personal matter. I promised the good *señor* I would not tell. But let us return to my present difficulty. Here I am, come to collect my nightly payment, according to my contract with the *ranchero,* and this little creature prevents me. Grab him by the shoulders so that I can pull myself free. Then I will go and get two chickens—one for you—and pass up my dinner tomorrow night."

The greedy coyote was excited at the thought of getting one of the *ranchero*'s celebrated hens without running the risk of being shot. He walked behind the wax figure and grabbed its shoulders with his paws.

Straightaway, Sister Fox pulled free of the wax. "Now you wait here while I get a chicken for each of us. Of course, I insist that you take the fatter one!"

So the foolish coyote waited, his paws on the wax figure and his mind on the fat hen that his cousin would soon bring him.

But the only one who came was Don Perez. He had been awakened by the squawking in his henhouse when Sister Fox snatched his finest hen and ran off into the night.

When he saw the coyote, he cried, *"¡Bandido!"* Then he fired his rifle. The shot went amiss and the wax figure exploded, allowing Brother Coyote to escape. But the unhappy creature had bits of wax stuck to his fur for days afterward. He vowed revenge upon Sister Fox for her scheming that had cost him a fine dinner, and—very nearly—his life.

Not long after this, it happened that Sister Fox stole a freshly baked loaf of bread from a house on the edge of town. As she was running away into the desert with her still-warm prize, she met her cousin in a little *arroyo*.

Brother Coyote was still very angry about the business with the wax man. He pounced upon the fox and bared his fangs at her. "Little cousin," he snarled, "if you do not give me that loaf of bread, I will gobble you up on the spot!"

"Oh," said the fox, thinking quickly, "this bread is not to eat. It is to lure the roosters—*¡Hay muchos!* There are so many!—that are kept in a certain *hacienda* I have discovered. Tonight I am going to steal as many as I have crumbs of bread."

"Well," said the gullible coyote, "let me go with you."

"No," said Sister Fox, "those roosters are so fat and lazy that they can barely move. Why should I share the secret with you?"

"Because," said the coyote unpleasantly, "I will devour you if you do *not* let me go with you."

"Well, all right," said the fox, "I will take the bread and run home now. When the moon has set, I will meet you here. *¡Adiós!*"

But Brother Coyote slapped a heavy paw across her tail. "To be certain that you do not run away, we will stay here together until the moon has set. And I am warning you: If we do not come away with ten times ten fat roosters tonight, you will not see the dawn."

So they lay side by side in the *arroyo* as the moon rose and set. By starlight, Sister Fox led her cousin to a huge wooden gate set in a high adobe wall.

"Here," she whispered.

"Hand over the bread *pronto,*" Brother Coyote ordered.

The fox took a bit of the bread and crumbled it into his paw, telling him, "The roosters are just inside this gate. Push open the latch. That will be easy for you because you are bigger and stronger than I am. As soon as you are inside, scatter these bread crumbs and call, 'Here, here, *Señor* Rooster, see what I have brought you.' Then you will get a reward beyond your wildest imagining. Just be sure your greediness does not make you forget your cousin who brought you here."

Eagerly Brother Coyote took the bread crumbs, stood up on his hind legs, and tugged and pushed until he opened the big latch on the gate. Then, slipping through, he began to toss bread crumbs right and left, calling softly, "Here, here, *Señor* Rooster, see what I have for you."

But, once again, his clever cousin had tricked him. The courtyard inside held sleeping dogs, not roosters! In a moment, Brother Coyote, crying "*¡Ay! Ay! Ay!*" fled through the gate with the hounds snapping at his heels. "Sister Fox!" he howled, but she did not hear. She had long since returned to her lair to finish the loaf of bread and plan more mischief.

As it happened, the coyote eluded the dogs—but not before he had received several painful bites on his flank and left a tuft of his tail in the jaws of the lead hound.

Licking his wounds in his own den, he once again vowed to make his cousin suffer tenfold for the pain and humiliation she had caused him.

Many nights later, he chanced upon Sister Fox as she sat crouched beside a deep pool of water, in the foothills near the town.

"Without a doubt, I am going to eat you this time," he growled.

"Well, if it must be so, then it must be so," she said, sounding not in the least worried. "I just hope that, when you have swallowed my miserable bones and stringy meat, you still have room for this cheese I am guarding. Behold what a beautiful cheese it is!"

Brother Coyote looked in the direction she was facing. To his surprise, he saw what seemed to be a huge, round cheese just below the surface of the water. Of course, it was only the reflection of the full moon, riding high overhead. But the greedy coyote saw only what Sister Fox—and his own stomach—wanted him to see.

"Who left such a fine cheese in the water?" he asked suspiciously.

Sister Fox answered, "The family who lives in the grand *hacienda* not far from here. They are giving a *fiesta* soon. Because the cheese is so big, and the *fiesta* is five days away, they put it in this cool water to keep it from spoiling. I found it quite by accident."

"Well, now you have lost it," said Brother Coyote. "With all that good cheese in easy reach, I will wait and gobble you up another time. *¡Vete!* Scram!"

"*¡Gracias!*" called Sister Fox as she scampered away. Then the greedy coyote jumped into the pond to pull out the cheese. But all he got for his efforts was wet fur and a bone-deep chill.

Shivering, his sopping tail dragging in the dust, he returned to his cave to plot a terrible revenge on his cousin.

▼    ▼    ▼

Their final, fatal meeting came when Brother Coyote chased Sister Fox into a canebrake and cornered her there.

"Now I am going to kill you and eat you, for all the misery you have caused me."

"That is fair," the fox replied. "But, listen! Let me help set things right, so that I can go to heaven with a clear conscience. I had not planned to tell anyone, but I was headed for this very place when you surprised me. You see," she said, lowering her voice to a whisper, "I have learned that a wedding party is coming this way. To reach the church, they must pass through this canebrake. The bride and groom are the children of very wealthy *hacendados*. Their servants carry chickens to roast, *tortillas, frijoles,* sweet cakes, and every manner of good thing to eat. Hidden beside the path here, I thought it would be easy to steal the best of what passes by."

"*¿De veras?*" asked the ever-hungry coyote, wanting to believe her wild story.

"*Sí,* it is true. Would I dare to tell you a lie," Sister Fox asked, "when you are going to send me to heaven today? San Pedro would not let me through the gate of pearls with a fresh sin on my soul."

"That's true enough," agreed Brother Coyote.

"My only fear," said the fox, "is that the people will take the second path through the canebrake, while we are watching this one. I will go and watch the other path. Then we must both listen for fireworks. That will mean the wedding party is coming. Whichever of us hears this must right away go and call the other, so that we will be ready for them."

"*¡Bueno!*" said the coyote, settling down to watch the path that wound through the tall, tinder-dry cane. He kept his ears up to listen for the sound of fireworks or Sister Fox's call.

"*¡Adiós!*" cried the sly fox, as she slipped out of the canebreak. Soon she returned, carrying in her jaws a burning brand from the kitchen of the *hacienda.* Using this, she set the canebrake on fire. When the blazing cane began to go *Pop! Popple! Pop!* the coyote mistook the sound for the noise of the wedding party's fireworks. He began to dance for joy, thinking of all the good food that he would soon have. He planned to take what he could for himself alone, and then he would punish his cousin.

The nearer the fire came and the louder the crackling and popping grew, the more wildly the coyote leaped and capered. "Ah, here they come, here they come!" he sang.

Too late, the foolish creature discovered that he was dancing not at a wedding, but at a funeral—his own!

# Women of the West

# Hekeke

## MIWOK

At one time the Miwok people comprised the largest nation within California, with over 100 villages. The course of history has reduced the Miwoks (which means simply "Humans," or "People") to a handful these days. The Coast Miwok inhabited the area of present-day San Francisco south to the area around Santa Barbara. The Central Miwok occupied the rich lands along the Stanislaus, Merced, and Tuolomne rivers in east-central California—an area that includes Yosemite National Park (the name *Yosemite* comes from another Miwok word, *u-zu'-mai-ti*, which means "grizzly bear").

The Wal'-li tribe (the name comes from the Miwok word *wal'-lim*, meaning "down below," which distinguishes them from the Yosemite tribes and others living higher up in the Sierras) lived in villages along the Merced and Tuolomne (from the place name *O-tūl'-wi-uh*) rivers. Each village was ruled by a male chief, but both women and men could become shamans, or healers. The Central Miwoks lived in simple, cone-shaped shelters of brushwood or bark. Acorns formed the staple of their diet, but they also ate seeds, sweet roots, wild plants, nuts, deer, fish, wild fowl, rabbits, grubs, and grasshoppers. They excelled at basket weaving, which supplied them with the means of gathering, preparing, and cooking foods (acorn soups and mush were heated in pitch-covered baskets into which heated stones were dropped). They even wore basketry hats, which were decorated with feathers from the redheaded woodpecker, the yellow warbler, and other birds.

Women traditionally wore aprons in front and back made of

shredded bark or plant fibers and robes made of rabbit skin. They cut their shiny black hair in straight bangs across the forehead, letting it grow long on either side.

---

MANY, MANY MOONS ago, a giant ogre, Yayali, lived in a cave above the South Fork of the Tuolumne River. Covered with shaggy hair, the monster hopped on one leg with a leather boot that came up above his single knee. He slept during the day, and at night he took a burden basket, a *chi-kele,* made of rock, and went hunting. He kidnapped men and women from the villages, for he was a cannibal. When he returned to his cave, he would gobble the unfortunates up, then fall asleep with a full belly.

Time and again, the Miwok people dug pits and covered them with brush to capture Yayali, but he always managed to avoid such traps. Sometimes the warriors would get close enough to shoot the monster's chest and arms so full of arrows that he looked like a porcupine—but nothing stopped the giant.

One night in early autumn, he chanced upon a woman of the Wal-li tribe, Hekeke, who had gone out with her people to gather acorns from the black oaks. But when the other men, women, and children had returned to their village, the exhausted Hekeke had fallen asleep in the forest. She awoke with a start when she heard the *thud-thud-thud* of the giant hopping on his single foot. Before she could gather her robe and burden basket, the monster leaped into view and spotted her. He gave a triumphant cry that shivered the leaves on the oaks.

Now Hekeke was a woman of unusual courage and intelligence. Unlike others who had fallen into Yayali's hands, she did not faint from fright upon seeing the misshapen giant towering above her. Instead, she asked in a loud voice, *"Wi'-oh u-kūh'?"* which meant, "How do you do?"

The monster, who was as dull witted as the woman was sharp-witted, did not know what to make of this human who spoke to him as if she were not afraid of him in the least. *"He'-kang-ma,"* Yayali answered at last, meaning, "I am hungry."

Still, the woman showed no fear, although, inside, fear clutched her heart with fingers of ice. "I have heard the old people say that you live in a great cave. They say that the opening is sealed with a rock so big that you alone are strong enough to move it. I would like to see these things before I die."

Eager to show off his dwelling place and his strength, Yayali said, "I will show you these things. Then I will eat you."

"That is as it must be," Hekeke said, refusing to let the trembling inside her reveal itself in her voice.

So he put her in his stone burden basket, which was supported by a strap of many deer hides twisted together that rested against his forehead. Then he carried her to his cave, high up in the hills.

She made a show of crying out in wonder when he rolled aside the stone in the entranceway and showed her his cave. Nor did she let him see how frightened she was as he kicked aside the piled-up bones of those unhappy Miwoks who had become his meals. But tears, which she quickly wiped away, came to her eyes. Among those bones, she was certain, were those of her husband, whom the giant had taken the year before.

She remembered how she had wept and wailed and daubed her face with pitch as a sign of mourning. But she showed nothing of what she was feeling to the monster. Recalling her lost husband, she felt anger drive all the fear out of her heart.

Then the brave and clever woman cried, "Poor Yayali!"

Surprised, the giant glared at her and said, "How dare you call me 'Poor Yayali'? I am the strongest being in the world. Men and women run away at the sight of me!"

"Forgive me," said the woman, hanging her head as though his words had shamed her. "I only think it is sad that such a powerful person must live in such a dirty cave. Look at those bones there! It is like a *cho-ko'-ni*, a doghouse."

" 'A doghouse'!" roared the monster. The sound of his anger booming off the walls of the cave forced Hekeke to press her hands against her ears to keep from going deaf.

Quickly she said, "A great being should have a wife. Her duty is to see that he is never ashamed of where he lives."

Her words soothed Yayali's anger. "You are right to point this out to me," he said. "I am far too great a person to live in a dog's place."

"I am young and strong," said Hekeke, "I could keep house for you."

Listening to her words and seeing how pretty she was, the giant decided to spare her. He made her his wife.

The first thing she did was take the bones and bury them in the manner of her people. Because the giant watched her all the time, she refused to let any tears betray her.

In the morning, Yayali watched Hekeke take the leaves of a soap-root plant to make a rude brush. This she used to sweep out the cave and its entranceway. But when the sun rose higher and the giant grew tired, he did not trust her to stay, so he rolled the stone across the cave entrance, trapping her inside. In the evening, when he went hunting, he did the same. So the woman was never able to escape, although she almost scraped the skin off her hands trying to push or pry the vast stone aside just far enough so that she could slip out.

Each time the cannibal brought back a victim, she begged him to spare the person.

"I will roast deer meat and cook acorn mash for you instead," she cried.

But Yayali only laughed at the idea. "This has been my only food since Coyote made the world." Then he pushed her aside and ate his terrible meal.

The poor woman lived on grasshoppers and grubs and pine nuts that she found for herself. Yayali sometimes brought her a hare to cook. She was grateful for this, because the meat gave her strength and kept up her spirits while she plotted to escape. After eating, she cut the skin into narrow strips and set them in the sun to dry. When she had enough, she tied the strips together with fiber threads and made a robe for herself, because it was always cold and damp in the cave. But just as often, the monster forgot to bring her anything at all to eat, and so she grew weak.

Hekeke never stopped trying to think of ways to slay the monster and escape. She noticed that he never took his one boot off, but she could not get him to tell her why. One day, while he was asleep, she slipped his boot off and discovered that the monster's heart, like a swelling of flesh, was right above his ankle. But she had grown so frail from lack of food, she did not have the strength to try to kill the creature herself. She put his boot back on and tried to decide what to do.

As it happened, several nights later, when the ogre left to hunt in the night, he forgot to seal the rock as tightly as he should. To her delight, Hekeke, who had shrunk to little more than skin and bones, was just able to slip out. As fast as her weakened body would allow, she ran back to her people. All the time, she listened for the dreaded *thud-thud-thud!* of Yayali's pursuit. But she reached the village safely.

There, while dogs barked and children cried out in fear, she called the sleepy Wal-li out of their brushwood shelters. Quickly she told them the giant's secret. Then, although she was terrified of putting herself back in Yayali's power, she offered to lead a war party to the cave.

Still the monster had not come back. To the warriors, Hekeke said, "You must hide in the cave. I will go inside myself. Then, when Yayali sleeps, we will kill him."

She slipped back into the cave, before the giant returned. Although all the men pushed together, they could not budge the stone; so only one fifteen-year-old boy, Et-tetti, could follow her through the narrow opening.

To the boy, Hekeke said, "When I show the giant's heart to you, you must kill him with your first arrow!"

Et-tetti said, "My bow is sturdy, and I have fletched my arrows with feathers from the red-tailed hawk. Each will find Yayali's heart the way a hawk drops on a rabbit."

"That is good!" Hekeke said. Then she hid him in one of the stone baskets that Yayali used for hunting. Next she set about sweeping the floor with a handful of reeds, because she had heard the *thud-thud-thud* of the giant returning. Soon he rolled the rock aside and entered the cave carrying a basket with two victims, a man and a woman, half fainting with fright. He pulled the rock across the entrance, fixing it so tightly that only smoke from Hekeke's cooking fire could escape.

"Poor Yayali," said Hekeke, "you seem tired from your hunting. Lie down. You will eat better if you rest." Holding a finger to her lips to silence the cries of the captured man and woman, Hekeke began to sing gently to lull Yayali to sleep.

Soon, the ogre fell into a doze. Then Hekeke, still singing, gently slipped off his boot, and signaled Et-tetti. The boy fired his arrow into the ogre's heart. Yayali abruptly rose up to full height and gave a bellow louder than a thunderclap. The terrible sound of his cry popped the great rock out of the cave mouth, but the falling monster tumbled down and smashed Hekeke and Et-tetti to a mere height of three feet.

The two were honored by their tribe for ridding the land of the man-eating monster. The Wal-li held a week-long celebration at which they served much deer meat, rabbit, fish from the river, acorn bread, roasted grasshoppers, and baskets of sweet roots and berries. All the men, women, and children danced, and many composed songs about the death of Yayali.

Curiously, neither Hekeke nor Et-tetti grew any taller or older after

Yayali fell on them; and they never could speak a word after this. Some Miwok say they can still be glimpsed in the Tuolumne forest: if one looks quickly over his or her shoulder, that person may see two small, silent beings who mean no harm and seek only to live in peace in the green shadows of the woods.

# Otoonah

## ESKIMO

Alaska's native peoples are part of the Eskimo peoples who live all around the North Pole—in Canada, Greenland, and Russia. They are all related through a common root language, although, over the years, different peoples have developed widely differing languages, cultures, and traditions. In the face of almost overwhelming odds—when they are challenged daily to survive—this hardy people serve as a constant reminder of the human will to endure. They point up the ability of women and men to carve out a life in even the harshest of natural settings. The stories they tell sometimes seem as grim and unrelenting as the Arctic winter; this is an outgrowth of the realities the Eskimos confront every day. But the tales also can reveal rich humor and the deep happiness that fills the soul when the spring thaw arrives and the people celebrate the fact that they have survived another winter to enjoy another summer.

The story that follows comes from Kodiak Island, which was settled by the Eskimo people called the Sugpiaq. The Sugpiaq also inhabit the peninsula that leads to the Aleutian chain. The tale reflects, in the struggles of its heroine, the battle for survival that has been the Eskimos' bitter heritage since their forebears first crossed the frozen Bering Strait from Asia to North America centuries ago.

IN THOSE DAYS of the past, there was an Eskimo family—the parents, two brothers, and a sister—who lived in a village near the ocean. Summer was nearly at an end, and bitter winter was coming soon. For one family, the hunting had been especially bad: they had found few edible plants and berries to store, and they had fewer fish and eggs to bury in the ground where they wouldn't spoil.

One day, the brothers sent their younger sister to gather driftwood from the beach near the family's sod house. While she was gone, the older brother, Nanoona, said to his parents, "There is not enough food for five people. We must send our sister away. She is weak and does not hunt, yet she eats our food. Soon my brother and I will grow too weak to hunt. Then we will all starve."

Next the younger brother, Avraluk, said, "Four can live when five cannot. We will row our sister across the sea to one of the islands and leave her there."

Sadly, the parents agreed to this.

When the girl, Otoonah, returned with an armful of wood, her brothers told her what they had decided. *"Ahpah!* Father! *Ahkah!* Mother!" the wretched girl cried. But her parents turned away and would not look at her. Then her brothers put her in the family's large sealskin boat and rowed her to an island below the horizon. There they left her with only the poorest caribou hide that the family owned and flints to start a fire.

For a long time, she did nothing but sob. All the time she stared in the direction where the sun rises and imagined she could see traces of the mainland. Over and over she sang,

> Oh poor me!
> Oh unhappy daughter!
> So sad am I, so sad
> And so lonely!

Finally, when her hunger grew too much to bear, she gathered seaweed from the shore to eat. Then, piling up stones, she made herself a tiny hut. She wrapped herself in the skin at night. When she awoke, she ate more seaweed. But she grew weaker and weaker.

Then, one night, in her makeshift shelter of stones, an old man came to her in a dream. "Walk to the west until you find a broad, swift-flowing stream beside sweet berry bushes. Drink two times from the water, but do not drink again. And do not eat even one berry. But you will find there one other thing that you may take away with you."

She awoke soon after this and walked for a long time over the stony ground until she found the broad, swift-flowing stream bordered with berry bushes.

Kneeling, she cupped her hands and drank. The first time she sipped the water, she felt her strength returning. The second time, she felt herself growing stronger still. Although she was still thirsty and hungry, she did as the old man in the dream had told her. She did not take a single drop more or taste a single ripe berry.

Looking across the current, she saw an *ulu*, a knife, with a carved ivory handle lying on a flat rock. With her newfound strength, she lifted a tree trunk and set it over the stream. Then she claimed the knife.

In the days that followed, she used the knife to make a bird spear, harpoon, and a bow and arrows for herself. She practiced throwing the spear and harpoon and shooting arrows until she became skilled at using these weapons.

At the same time, she explored the island and discovered that it was a plentiful hunting ground, with ptarmigans and hares and seals that would sun themselves on the rocks. So she was able to provide plenty of food for herself. Then she made herself clothing, boots, and a cape of sealskin that she had scraped and stretched on the ground to dry. As the days grew cold, she even built a kayak.

Sitting by herself in the warmth of her hut, over which she had packed dirt and which was filled with furs, she often dreamed of sailing home across the sea. She vowed to punish her brothers and her parents who had abandoned her so heartlessly.

Ice began to form on ponds and on the sea. Otoonah could no longer take her kayak out because the ice would pierce its skin cover. Snow fell and piled up against the hut; winds began to howl across the island. But she had plenty of dried seal meat and fish. Inside the shelter it was warm, lit by the yellow flame of a lamp that she had carved from soapstone. The wick was made of moss, and the basin was filled with oil from blubber that she had chewed to release the fuel. Several dried seal stomachs hung on the wall, holding more oil.

When the storms were at their worst and she was weathered in, the young woman sat on her bed platform covered with shrubs and skins and sang songs. Some she remembered her mother singing to her; some she made up: happy songs about summer warmth, bitter songs about loneliness, or boastful songs that she would someday sing when she returned well fed to mock her starving family.

The long Arctic night arrived. At noon, the sun—too weary to climb above the horizon—spread the thin light of false dawn over a world blanketed with snow and ice.

Now the young woman hunted seals by finding one of their breathing holes in the icebound sea. She would pile up blocks of snow and sit motionlessly. When she heard a seal snort, she would instantly plunge her harpoon straight down, haul the unhappy creature onto the ice, and finish it off.

In time, she recognized the promise of spring as the first rays of sunlight touched the highest peaks far inland. Although terrible cold still gripped the island, the coming of daylight made hunting easier. Soon the ice mass covering the sea began to break apart into smaller floes.

▼　▼　▼

One day, approaching her favorite hunting area, the young woman heard human voices. At first the sound alone startled her. She was even more astounded to discover that she knew those voices. Running forward, she met her brothers, who were just beaching their kayaks on the shore. At the sight of them, the young woman forgot all her thoughts of revenge.

They two men raised their harpoons at the sight of this strange person running toward them. But they lowered them when they heard her call out, "Nanoona! Avraluk! I am your sister. I am Otoonah!"

Hungry for the sound of human voices, she asked them many questions about her old home and her parents. But they merely shrugged and spoke a few words. They could only stare at the fine furs she wore and the glow of well-fed, good health in her face.

"What man has given you so much food and such fine furs?" her older brother demanded.

"Your husband must give us a portion of what he has," said her younger brother, "since he has married our sister."

Angrily, she said, "No man has given me anything. What I have I have been given by the Old Woman of the Sea who let me take some of the seals and fish in her keeping."

"No woman is such a good hunter," said her older brother. Then they both laughed at her.

"If you are such a hunter," Nanoona continued, "I would challenge you to a hunt."

"And I," Avraluk added.

Angered by their laughter, the young woman said, "I accept your challenge."

They waited until she had launched her own kayak. Then they zigzagged swiftly amid the ice floes. Soon each was lost to the sight of the other.

For the young woman, the hunting was good. By the time she returned, she had two seals lashed to the narrow deck of her kayak. As she rowed with her single paddle which she held in the middle, dipping first right and then left, she sang a little song of thanksgiving to the Old Woman of the Sea.

Both her brothers returned much later, angry and empty-handed. She was already roasting some meat when they came to her hut. She invited them to share her food and spend the night. She did not mock them because she knew they were chewing on bitter defeat with every mouthful of her meat—even as she was savoring her victory. When they had finished eating, they did not thank her. They sat apart and whispered together.

In the morning, she awoke and discovered that her brothers were gone. They had also stolen her ivory-handled *ulu* in the fish-skin pouch she had made for it, and most of her furs and meat. Running to the shore, she saw the two of them far out to sea.

Angry at this second betrayal, she pursued them. She was stronger than either of them; and her boat was sturdier and swifter. Soon she overtook them. She shook her harpoon and cried, "Return what you have stolen, or I will gut your kayaks as I would a fish."

The two were cowards and quickly surrendered the stolen goods. Then the young woman laughed at *them*. To the shamefaced men, it sounded as though her laughter had been picked up by the roaring wind. Soon the sky itself was roaring with dark laughter, as a terrible storm arose.

The young woman, her goods safely tied down, paddled quickly back toward the island through a heavy sea. She called to her brothers to come back with her, but they ignored her. Stubbornly, they paddled on into the heart of the storm. Soon, she heard their calls for help as loud and forlorn as petrels' cries. But although she turned around and tried to find them, they had vanished beneath the waves.

Barely escaping with her own life, she reached safe harbor. For a day and a night she huddled in her shelter, until the wind blew itself out.

When the storm subsided, the young woman took as much meat as she could carry. Then she rowed across to her old village. There she found her parents grieving for their lost sons and fearful that they would soon starve with no one to provide for them.

Their grief turned to amazement when they saw Otoonah, her arms laden with food, coming up the beach toward them.

*"Punnick!* Daughter! Have you come home?" her father asked.

"I have come back because it is time for me to return," Otoonah said. "I will give you food from now on." So happy was she to be home that when she searched her heart, she found there no wish to hurt her parents any longer.

After this, she brought all her goods from the island and built herself a new hut, very close to the one in which her parents lived. She soon proved herself the best hunter in the village. Then she was sought by many men, each of whom wanted her to become his wife.

But she set her heart on one man, Apatasok. However, he alone would have no part of her because she insisted on taking a man's role in the hunt. "A woman is supposed to take care of the hunter," he said, "and watch out for his clothes. No more."

"Still, I am determined to have you for my husband," Otoonah said stubbornly.

"A girl does not take a husband of her own choosing. Her parents should seek a husband for her."

Then he walked away before she could argue any more.

However, the following winter, when they were hunting near each other on the edge of the frozen sea, Apatasok killed a seal. But while he was loading it on his sled, he discovered to his dismay that the scent of the kill had drawn a polar bear.

Quick-thinking Otoonah cut the traces on her own sled dogs and sent them to harass the bear. Then, with a cry of encouragement to her fellow hunter, she charged behind them, brandishing her harpoon.

The bear fought the dogs with its paws and teeth. Two dogs were felled by crushing blows. But the beast could not move because the circling huskies would attack at every opening. The young man rushed forward, trying to spear the bear in its heart. But the bear turned sharply, its paw shattering the hunter's spear and tumbling the man into the snow. The angered bear turned toward the man to finish him off. But, at that instant, the young woman charged forward, putting all of her weight behind her harpoon. The weapon pierced the bear's heart, and it dropped on the spot.

When the young man got to his feet and stared at the young woman standing beside the slain creature, he began to laugh. But the woman recognized that he was laughing because he was still alive, and because here was an unlooked-for supply of meat, and because he saw the foolishness of his refusal to marry a woman who hunted as well as any man.

Soon she was laughing, too.

When they returned to the village, they were wed. And the polar bear meat provided a marriage feast for their families and neighbors. Afterwards, they became a familiar sight as they hunted together, paddling their kayaks side by side.

# Hiiaka

## HAWAIIAN

Hiiaka is the beautiful youngest sister and favorite of Pele, the great fire goddess who lives in the molten heart of Hawaii's Kilauea Volcano. Pele rules over a family of fire gods, including Hiiaka and their brother, Lono-makua. While Pele is easily angered and quick to punish offenders with fiery eruptions of lava, Hiiaka is calm and kind and always ready to help humanity. Though she can be fierce when battling the dragon-like *mo'o* monsters, Hiiaka's greatest gifts are creative: she is a healer and the one who taught the people of Hawaii the arts of the hula, lei-making, and composing the long chants that are some of the finest examples of Hawaii's oral folklore tradition.

ONE DAY HAWAII's powerful fire goddess, Pele, sent for her sister, Hiiaka, who was wandering amid groves of scarlet-blossomed *'ohi'a* trees, far from the barren black lava fields and blazing fire pits of her home. The young goddess returned to Kilauea Volcano at once and sought her sister, Pele, who commanded her, "Find my beloved Lohiau, who has been stolen away by evil spirits."

Now Hiiaka knew that what her sister was asking involved great danger. But she knew how much her sister loved the mortal, who was chief of a distant island; and she had a great affection for Pele, who had always shown her special favor. So she said, "You are my dearest sister and truest friend. I will find Lohiau and scorn the perils of the journey."

But Hiiaka's loyal and courageous words hid the uneasiness she felt. She, too, had looked upon Lohiau with loving eyes. Because he was promised to Pele, she had denied her longing. But thoughts of him came often to her. So she had vowed to do everything in her power to keep apart from him. Now, commanded to go to his aid, she feared that the greatest danger lay not on the path ahead, but in her own heart.

Pele sensed nothing of Hiiaka's disquiet. To aid her sister on her quest, she gifted Hiiaka with a magical *pa-u*, a skirt that held the power of lightning in its folds. She traveled with Pau-o-palae (whose name means "skirt of palai fern"), her *kahu*, guardian servant. The goddess of ferns, Pau-o-palae provided Hiiaka with a beautiful robe woven of ferns.

Together they set out on their great adventure. Their route took them beyond a beach of black lava sands into a dense forest, where they met Pana-ewa, a witch-*mo'o* in the form of a huge reptile. The evil creature could take many forms. Alerted by her brothers who were little birds, the monster blocked Hiiaka's path.

"Why have you brought me no *awa* to drink, no *taro* and red fish to eat, no *tapas* for mats?" she challenged. "Had you brought such gifts, I would not bar your way."

"Pana-ewa, stand aside!" commanded Hiiaka.

"There is no way for you to pass," hissed Pana-ewa. "I will kill you. I will swallow you."

Then she laughed and called up fog and rain and wind to drive Hiiaka back. From the depths of the jungle, the *mo'o* summoned forth *eepas*, gnomelike beings, and many other vicious forest creatures to torment the travelers. Finally, tiring of the game, Pana-ewa herself attacked the goddess in her fog-body, choking her with tentacles of chill mist. But Hiiaka shook her magic skirt, threw the demon back with lightning bolts, and scattered the mist.

Next Pana-ewa took the form of freezing rain, then of a mighty wind that hurled trees at Hiiaka. But the goddess used the power of her lightning skirt to shatter the trunks and drive the monster back again. Pana-ewa fled deep into the forest, while Hiiaka took the opportunity to rest and regain her strength.

But the wicked one sent all sorts of horrible creatures against her. They ambushed Hiiaka at every turn and took a multitude of disguises. A withered bush, a bunch of grass, a moss-grown stone—any of these might suddenly spit venom or tear at the goddess with hook and claw. She drove them all away with the power of her bamboo knife and lightning skirt. Beside her, Pau-o-palae fought just as bravely.

Soon both were nearly dead from wounds and weariness—so tired that they could barely move. With her last breath, Hiiaka called for her sister, Pele, to help.

Her cry rolled like thunder across mountain and valley and stream to reach Pele, ever watchful in her fiery lake.

Angered, Pele sent a lightning storm that burned up Hiiaka's enemies in the forest. Then rain came in torrents, flooding the valleys with red water, sweeping Pana-ewa and her cohorts out to sea, where they were devoured by sharks.

Hiiaka's journey next took her to a lovely place of cloud-capped mountains and flowing rivers. There the goddesses of lightning and ferns met the human Wahine-omao, whose name means the "light-colored woman." Awed to be in the presence of such a powerful figure as Hiiaka, the woman threw herself on the ground before the goddess. But Hiiaka saw that she she was a person with an honest, generous heart, as well as brave and beautiful. So she invited her to join her on her quest.

The three—the two goddesses and Wahine-omao—swam across to the island called Hilo. At a hut on a bluff overlooking the shore, two girls—sisters—offered them dried fish and a little calabash full of *poi* porridge. Quickly, the three visitors sensed that the girls were distressed about something.

"What troubles you so?" asked Hiiaka.

"We are fearful for our father," said the first girl.

Her sister continued, "He took his canoe out last night, and he has not returned."

Hiiaka walked to the edge of the cliff. She looked first far out to sea, then down to where the waves crashed on the shore below. There she discovered the spirit of the girls' father wandering the shore.

Warning the others that they must not shed a single tear, Hiiaka climbed down the cliff face and attempted to capture the wandering spirit. She planned to force it back into the body of the fisherman, which lay on the shore where the sea had washed it up.

But the ghost tried to elude her. "Let me go," the spirit pleaded. "I will have a brighter and happier life among the trees and ferns of the forest."

Finally, Hiiaka used her "strong hand of Kilauea"—the power that belonged to her as one of the divine family living in the fire pit of Kilauea Volcano—to catch the spirit. Hiiaka also had vast powers of healing. Now she poured fresh water from a nearby stream over the body, while she chanted:

Here is the water of life.
*E ala e!* Awake! Arise!
Let life return.
The power of death is over.
It is lifted,
It has flown away.

At last, the ghost was compelled to reenter the body through its eyes and nose. Breath returned; the body stirred; the fisherman lived again.

The goddess and her companions continued their search, which grew ever more dangerous.

She had to fight Mo'o-lau, the dragon, who had enslaved the people who lived along the coast of of yet another island. The dragon boasted,

124

"You have no path through my lands unless you have great strength."

Haiiaka accepted his challenge. She fought with the power of her lightning *pa-u*, while he struck at her with his swift-moving tail and tried to grab her with his mighty jaws. Both had powerful magic to call upon, and again and again they fought each other to a standstill. But, at last, the goddess prevailed. She destroyed Mo'o-lau and the lesser dragons who had rallied to the monster's call for help.

Pau-o-palae, the goddess of ferns, met the chief of the people who had been enslaved by the dragons but were now free. They fell in love and were married. Then Pau-o-palae remained with her husband, while Hiiaka and Wahine-omao continued their search for Lohiau.

Hiiaka also had to drive away Mahiki, the whirlwind, and slay Makakiu, the sea serpent, before she finally crossed the sea in an outrigger canoe to the island, Maui, where Lohiau was kept in a mountain cave guarded by dragon women, enemies of Pele. These creatures raised a terrible storm, wrapped the mountains in freezing, clinging fog, and sent down avalanches of rock.

But Hiiaka fought past all these dangers. The final battle took place in a forested valley in front of the cave. There, at first, the goddess was almost defeated because the dragon women seemed able to survive the terrible power of her lightning. But again she used her magical "strong hand of Kilauea." This time, she caused the very trees and plants to come alive, twisting and twining roots and branches and vines around the dragon women. Then Hiiaka caused the hapless creatures to be hurled down the cliffs, where their bodies were broken into pieces on the rocks below.

At that instant, the storm quieted and the fog lifted. Then Hiiaka called forth Lohiau from the cave. She embraced him as a brother and began making preparations for the long journey home. Though the fire of love in her heart threatened to consume her, she resolved to keep the secret from Lohiau and remain loyal to Pele.

But Pele, in the fire pit of Kilauea, had first grown impatient, then furious as the days had passed without Hiiaka bringing Lohiau back to her.

"Where is my sister? Why has she not returned?" demanded the jealous goddess. As her anger grew, she cried out, "It must be that my faithless sister and Lohiau have fallen in love. They have forgotten me!"

Indeed, the young man *had* become charmed by Hiiaka, yet the girl remained faithful to Pele. But before she could escort Lohiau back to Kilauea, an enraged Pele caused the volcano to erupt. She stamped the floor of the fire pit so hard that the crater convulsed and the land trembled for miles around. Finally, she loosed a seething, bubbling, hissing flood of lava to burn up the land and all living things. The sky turned red as her anger turned into fire clouds—boiling fountains of flame and cinder—that shot up to the very curve of heaven; and the air was filled with the explosions of flaming gas called "Pele's curses"; and hot stones fell like rain on the tortured earth.

Fearful, Hiiaka hid herself and her companions on a small island. Then she sent Wahine-omao to Pele to act as messenger and calm her sister's anger. But the fire goddess imprisoned the unhappy woman in a cave and would not listen to her story.

Then Pele summoned her brother, Lono-makua, who has charge over the earth fires. She commanded him, "Go. Find the unfaithful couple. Kindle volcanoes around them and burn them to ashes."

Lono-makua did as he was commanded. Fountains of fire burst from the earth and ringed Hiiaka and Lohiau on their tiny island refuge. Although the terrible heat and flames could not hurt Hiiaka, the fire streams of lava instantly turned Lohiau to a shrunken figure of stone, and his spirit fled to a cool forest on a distant mountain.

Hiiaka, devastated by the death of Lohiau and the betrayal by her sister, became crazed with sorrow and anger. She began to hurl lightning bolts at the walls of Kilauea. She planned to break down the sides of the crater, so that the sea might pour through into the fire pit.

Then Pele realized that Hiiaka intended to fill the pit with water, so that her fires would be imprisoned and drowned. Pele's home would be destroyed, just as the monster Kama-puaa had once ruined Ka-lua-Pele (The Pit of Pele), her former home, with torrents of rain. Fearing that she would again be driven from her dwelling place, Pele looked for a way to turn aside her sister's wrath.

She released Wahine-omao from her prison and listened to her story. Then, filled with regret, she sent the human back to Hiiaka to calm her.

This Wahine-omao did, gently reminding Hiiaka, "Surely you can return Lohiau's ghost to his body, as you once returned the spirit of the drowned fisherman."

Indeed, this is what happened. Hiiaka repeated the ceremonies and prayers and called back her beloved's spirit from the distant forest. Upon the lifeless, stone form of Lohiau, she poured out water from a calabash, crying,

> Here's water, the Water of Life!
> Grant life in abundance, life!
> I pray thee awake!
> Here am I, Hiiaka.
> Awake, I beg and entreat thee!
> Let my prayer speed its way!

With a cry of joy, she saw the cold and withered form gain fullness, warmth, and color. There was a sudden rush of air into Lohiau's lungs; his eyelids flickered; he sat up. Gently Hiiaka and Wahine-omao led him to the ocean shore. There all three performed the ritual washing that removed the uncleanness of death. And when they emerged from the sunlit waves, each seemed to glow with a fresh and radiant beauty.

At last Pele and Hiiaka were reconciled. Pele realized that her sister was deeply in love with Lohiau—yet would never betray her. And she saw with sorrow, now, instead of anger, that Lohiau's eyes burned with love for Hiiaka. So Pele put aside her claim on the man, and Hiiaka and Lohiau were wed. And Wahine-omao became the wife of Lono-makua. But Hiiaka found that her adventures and her love for Lohiau had forever changed her. She could not take her former place in Pele's service at Kilauea.

She set sail for the island of Kauai, the land that Lohiau claimed as his own. There she was eventually joined by her faithful attendants, Pau-o-palae and Wahine-omao, their husbands, and certain of her sisters.

Many other adventures lay in wait for the brave and much-beloved goddess whom the islander people still refer to in song as *Hiiaka—ka no'iau—i ka poli o Pele*, "Hiiaka, the wise, the darling of Pele."

But those tales are for another telling.

# Sources

EPIGRAPH
From "Voyageur Songs of the Missouri" (copyright, 1954, by Missouri Historical Society, St. Louis; reprinted in B. A. Botkin, ed., *A Treasury of Mississippi River Folklore: Stories, Ballads, Traditions and Folkways of the Mid-American River Country,* New York: Bonanza Books, 1978), one of many such songs sung by the early French explorers in the Louisiana territory and French Canada. These can be traced back to the 1800s.

THE STAR MAIDEN
Adapted from a tale in Lewis Spence, *North American Indians: Myths and Legends Series* (George G. Harrap & Co., 1914); reprinted, London: Bracken Books, 1985. See also: *Tales of the North American Indians,* selected and annotated by Stith Thompson (Bloomington: Indiana University Press, 1929, 1966).

Additional details on Chippewa life and lore came from collateral sources such as Basil Johnston's *Ojibway Heritage,* Toronto: McClelland and Stewart, 1976; reprinted, Lincoln, Nebraska: University of Nebraska Press, 1990); Ruth Murray Underhill's *Red Man's America: A History of Indians in the United States,* rev. ed. (Chicago: The University of Chicago Press, 1953, 1971); Colin F. Taylor's *The Native Americans: The Indigenous People of North America* (New York: Smithmark Publishers Inc., 1991); and numerous other volumes.

BESS CALL
Consult *The Parade of Heroes: Legendary Figures in American Lore from Journals and Archives of American Folklore and Culture,* selected and edited by Tristram Potter Coffin and Hennig Coffin (New York: Anchor Press/Doubleday, 1978). Also mentioned in Harold W. Thompson, *Body, Boots & Britches: Folktales, Ballads and Speech from Country New*

*York* (New York: J. B. Lippincott Company, 1939; reprinted, New York: Dover Publications, Inc., 1962).

DROP STAR

Primary sources include the editors of *Life, The Life Treasury of American Folklore: Including a Comprehensive Guide to Persons, Places, and Events,* with paintings by James Lewicki (Time Incorporated, 1961); and *Myths and Legends of Our Own Land* by Charles M. Skinner (New York: J. B. Lippincott Company, 1896). Details on tribes of the area came from a variety of sources, including the Holland Land Office Museum, Holland County, New York.

ANNIE CHRISTMAS

This character first makes an appearance in Lyle Saxon, Robert Tallant, and Edward Dreyer, eds., *Gumbo Ya-Ya: A Collection of Louisiana Folk Tales,* published in 1945 by the Louisiana Library; reprinted by Bonanza Books, New York, n.d. Her story also appears in numerous collections, including *American Folklore and Legend: The Saga of Our Heroes and Heroines, Our Braggers, Boosters and Bad Men, Our Beliefs and Superstitions* by the editors of *Reader's Digest* (Pleasantville, New York: The Reader's Digest Association, Inc., 1978). A version in M. A. Jagendorf's *Folk Stories of the South* (New York: The Vanguard, Press, Inc., 1972) notes that "White folks say she was a white woman, and black folks say she was black as shining coal." But the truth—insofar as legends and tall tales have their "truth"—is that Annie was black, no two ways about it.

MOLLY COTTONTAIL

Adapted from a narrative in Anne Virginia Culbertson (b. 1864), *At the Big House: Where Aunt Nancy and Aunt 'Phrony Held Forth on the Animal Folks,* illustrated by E. Warde Blaisdell (Indianapolis: The Bobbs-Merrill Co., 1905). I have also consulted a variety of parallel texts, including a story from Virginia collected by A. M. Bacon and Elsie Clews Parsons in *The Journal of Folklore,* vol. 35, 1922, in which a female rabbit (unnamed in the brief tale, but presumably Molly) tricks Mr. Bear and actually gets him to agree to play "riding horse" and carry her to a party. Clearly the "female trickster" story does survive widely, if in a scattered fashion.

SUSANNA AND SIMON

Retold from "The Adventures of Simon and Susanna," in "Uncle Remus" (Joel Chandler Harris), *Daddy Jake, the Runaway: And Short Stories Told After Dark* (New York: The Century Company, 1889).

SAL FINK

Major sources include Jane Polley, ed., *American Folklore and Legend* (Pleasantville, New York: The Reader's Digest Association, Inc., 1978), drawn from B. A. Botkin, *A*

*Treasury of Mississippi River Folklore* (op. cit.) accounts reprinted in *Half Horse Half Alligator: The Growth of the Mike Fink Legend*, edited with an introduction and notes by Walter Blair and Franklin J. Meine (Chicago: University of Chicago Press, 1956; reprinted, Lincoln, Nebraska: University of Nebraska Press/Bison Books, 1981), and *Ring-tailed Roarers: Tall Tales of the American Frontier 1830–60*, edited with an introduction by V.L.O. Chittick (Caldwell, Idaho: The Caxton Printers, Ltd., 1943).

### SWEET BETSEY FROM PIKE
For a look at the original words and music of this ballad, the reader should consult Richard A. Dwyer and Richard E. Lingenfelter, *The Songs of the Gold Rush*, music edited with guitar arrangements by David Cohen (Berkeley: University of California Press, 1964). Additional key resources for this retelling include the prose synopsis in *The Life Treasury of American Folklore* (op. cit.); *Sweet Betsey from Pike: A Song from the Gold Rush Days*, arranged and illustrated by Robert Andrew Parker (New York: Viking, 1978); and Julia Cooley Altrocchi's vivid retracing of pioneer journeys in *The Old California Trail: Traces in Folklore and Furrow* (Caldwell, Idaho: The Caxton Printers, Ltd., 1945).

### OLD SALLY CATO
Suggested by a narrative in Earl A. Collins, *Legends and Lore of Missouri*, with photographs by Garland Fronabarger (San Antonio: The Naylor Company, 1951). Other stories with similar elements that were consulted include "How Toodie Fixed Old Grunt," originally published in Vance Randolph's *The Devil's Pretty Daughter: And Other Ozark Folktales* (New York: Columbia University Press, 1955), retold in Suzanne I. Barchers' *Wise Women: Folk and Fairy Tales from Around the World* (Englewood, Colorado: Libraries Unlimited, 1990); "Sody Sallyraytus," in Richard Chase's *Grandfather Tales: American-English Folk Tales* (Boston: Houghton-Mifflin Company, 1948); and the brief narrative, "Bum, Bum, Sally Lum," included in an article on "Tennessee Tall Tales" in the *Tennessee Folklore Society Bulletin* (Murfreesboro, Tennessee: The Tennessee Folklore Society, Vol. V, No. 3, October, 1939). For an example of the African "root tale," see "Mahada and the Bull Elephant," in *Some Gold and a Little Ivory: Country Tales from Ghana and the Ivory Coast*, edited by Edythe Rance Haskett (New York: The John Day Company, 1971). See also the discussion in *Afro-American Folktales: Stories from Black Traditions in the New World*, selected and edited by Roger D. Abrahams (New York: Pantheon Books, 1985).

### PALE-FACED LIGHTNING
Based on a brief account in Charles M. Skinner, *Myths and Legends of Our Own Land*, originally published by J. B. Lippincott Company, New York, in 1896. I have intermingled details of Pueblo life from a variety of sources, including John Upton Terrell's *Pueblos, Gods and Spaniards* (New York: The Dial Press, 1973); Paul Horgan's

*Heroic Triad: Essays in the Social Energies of Three Southwestern Cultures* (rev. ed., New York: Holt, Rinehart and Winston, 1970); Bertha P. Dutton's *American Indians of the Southwest* (Albuquerque: University of New Mexico Press, 1975, 1983); and Natalie Curtis, *The Indians Book: Authentic Native American Legends, Lore & Music,* originally published in 1905, reprinted by Bonanza Books in 1987. An intriguing parallel turned up in Edwina B. Doran's essay, "The Rock Woman and the Little People—White County Legends," in the *Tennessee Folklore Society Bulletin,* Vol. L, No. 4, Winter, 1984, Murfreesboro, Tennessee: Tennessee Folklore Society. The author discusses the local belief that in the time of the Mound Builders, there existed a race of little people or pygmies, and that the body of one—a well-formed woman described as "small but not childlike"—had survived in petrified state and had been uncovered in a field in 1903. For a fuller discussion of the evidence concerning "Who Discovered America?" one might refer to the chapter of that title in Peter Haining's *Ancient Mysteries* (Richmond, Victoria, Australia: Hutchinson of Australia, 1977).

### POHAHA

Retold from a brief account in Elsie Clews Parsons, "The Social Organization of the Tewa of New Mexico," in *Memoirs of the American Folklore Society,* vol. 36, 1929, which is also included, in somewhat shortened form, in Carolyn Niethammer, *Daughters of the Earth: The Lives and Legends of American Indian Women* (New York: Collier Macmillan, 1977). Additional crucial information on Tewa culture and history: Gertrude Prokosch Kurath with Antonio Garcia *Music and Dance of the Tewa Pueblos* (Museum of New Mexico Research Records, no. 8, Santa Fe: Museum of New Mexico Press, 1970); Ruth M. Underhill, *Red Man's America: A History of Indians in the United States* (rev. ed., Chicago: University of Chicago Press, 1953, 1971); and Natalie Curtis, ed., *The Indians' Book: Authentic Native American Legends, Lore & Music* op. cit.

### SISTER FOX AND BROTHER COYOTE

Composited and rewritten from various sources, including John O. West, *Mexican-American Folklore: Legends, Songs, Festivals, Proverbs, Crafts, Tales of Saints, of Revolutionaries, and More* (Little Rock: August House, Inc., 1988); *Literary Folklore of the Hispanic Southwest,* gathered and interpreted by Aurora Lucero-White Lea (San Antonio: The Naylor Company, 1953); and Riley Aiken, *Mexican Tales from the Borderland: From the Publications of the Texas Forklore Society,* illustrations by Dennis Zamora (Dallas: Southern Methodist University Press, 1980).

### HEKEKE

Adapted and expanded from a legend recorded in G. Ezra Dane in collaboration with Beatrice J. Dane, *Ghost Town: Wherein Is Told Much That Is Wonderful, Laughable and Tragic, and Some That Is Hard to Believe, About Life During the Gold Rush and Later in the Town of Columbia on California's Mother Lode, as Remembered by the Oldest Inhabitants and Here for the First Time Set Down* (reprinted, New York: Tudor Publishing Company, 1948). Details of Miwok language, history, and culture come from Stephen Powers's classic, *Tribes of California* (originally published in 1877; reprinted, Berkeley: University of California Press, 1976). Younger readers in particular might want to seek out the brief, but also very helpful, Fran Hubbard, *A Day with Tupi: An Indian Boy of the Sierra*, illustrated by Ed Vella (Fresno: The Awani Press, 1955). Other noteworthy sources include Ruth M. Underhill, *Red Man's America* (Chicago: The University of Chicago Press, 1953, 1971) and James J. Rawls, *Indians of California: The Changing Image* (Norman, Oklahoma: University of Oaklahoma Press, 1984), which traces the prejudice and ignorance that distorted the way in which Native Californians were viewed and helped foster their decimation at the hands of European and American newcomers.

OTOONAH

Based on a legend from Kodiak Island, Alaska, outlined in Maria Wiegle's *Spiders and Spinsters: Women and Mythology* (Albuquerque: University of New Mexico Press, 1982). Details of Eskimo history and culture came from collateral readings that include Franz Boas's account, "An Eskimo Winter," in *American Indian Life*, edited by Elsie Clews Persons (originally published, Lincoln: University of Nebraska Press, 1922, 1967; reprinted, New York: Arlington House, Inc., 1983); Edward A. Tennant and Joseph N. Bitar, eds., *Yupik Lore: Oral Traditions of an Eskimo People* (a joint publication of Bethel, Alaska: Lower Kuskokwim School District; and Albuquerque, New Mexico: Educational Research Associates, 1981); Franz Boas's *The Central Eskimo* (Washington, D.C.: The Smithsonian Institution; reprinted, Lincoln: University of Nebraska Press/Bison Books, 1964); and *The Girl Who Married a Ghost: And Other Tales from the North American Indian*, collected, and with photographs, by Edward S. Curtis, edited by John Bierhorst (New York: Four Winds Press, 1978). See also my *Song of Sedna*, illustrated by Daniel San Souci (New York: Delacorte/Doubleday, 1981).

HIIAKA

Retold from versions of the myth found in the following volumes: *Hawaiian Legends of Volcanoes*, collected and translated from the Hawaiian by William D. Westervelt, first published in 1916, reprinted, Rutland, Vermont: Charles E. Tuttle Company, Inc., 1963; it is still considered a pioneering study of Hawaiian folklore; Nathaniel B. Emerson, *Pele and Hiiaka: A Myth from Hawaii*, originally published in 1915; reprinted with a new introduction and photographs, Rutland, Vermont: Charles E. Tuttle Company, Inc., 1978; and Martha Beckwith, *Hawaiian Mythology*, originally published by Yale University Press for the Folklore Foundation of Vassar College, 1940; reprinted, Honolulu: the University of Hawaii Press, 1970. Numerous other sources of Hawaiian mythology, natural history, and lore were also consulted.

# Bibliography

Adams, Kathleen, and Atchinson, Frances Elizabeth, compilers. *A Book of Princess Stories*. New York: Dodd, Mead and Company, Inc., 1927; reprinted, New York: Derrydale Books/Crown Publishers, Inc., 1987.

Aikman, Duncan. *Calamity Jane and the Lady Wildcats*. Lincoln: University of Nebraska Press/Bison Books, 1927, 1954, 1987.

Allen, Paula Gunn. *Grandmothers of the Light: A Medicine Woman's Sourcebook*. Boston: Beacon Press, 1991.

Allen, Paula Gunn. *Spider Woman's Granddaughters: Traditional Tales of Contemporary Writing by Native American Women*. Boston: Beacon Press, 1989; reprinted, New York: Fawcett Books, 1990.

Ann, Martha, and Myers, Dorothy Imel. *Goddesses in World Mythology: A Biographical Dictionary*. New York: Oxford University Press, 1993.

Ashwell, James R.; Julia Wilhoit; Jennette Edwards; and Other Members of the Tennessee Writers' Project. *God Bless the Devil! Liar's Bench Tales*. Chapel Hill: University of North Carolina Press, 1940.

Auerbach, Nina, and Knoepflmacher, U. C., eds. *Forbidden Journeys: Fairy Tales and Fantasies by Victorian Women Writers*. Chicago: The University of Chicago Press, 1992.

Baring, Anne, and Cashford, Jules. *The Myth of the Goddess: Evolution of an Image*. New York: Penguin Putnam Inc., 1991.

Battle, Kemp P. *Great American Folklore: Legends, Tales, Ballads and Superstitions from All Across America*. New York: Doubleday and Company, Inc., 1986.

Baum, L. Frank. *American Fairy Tales;* reprint of a text originally published by Chicago: George M. Hill Company, 1901; reprinted, New York: Dover Publications, Inc., 1978.

Bell, Robert E. *Women of Classical Mythology: A Biographical Dictionary*. New York: Oxford University Press, 1991.

Bennett, Gillian. *Traditions of Belief: Women, Folklore and the Supernatural Today*. New York: Viking Penguin, Inc., 1987.

Berger, Pamela. *The Goddess Obscured: Transformation of the Grain Protectress from Goddess to Saint*. Boston: Beacon Press, 1985.

Bettelheim, Bruno. *The Use of Enchantment: The Meaning and Importance of Fairy Tales*. New York: Knopf, 1976.

Bierhorst, John. *The Mythology of North America*. New York: William Morrow and Company, Inc., 1985.

Blair, Walter. *Tall Tale America: A Legendary History of Our Humorous Heroes*. New York: Coward-McCann Inc., 1944.

Blashfield, Jean F. *Hellraisers, Heroines and Holy Women: Women's Most Remarkable Contributions to History*. New York: St. Martin's Press, 1981.

Botkin, B. A. *A Treasury of American Folklore: Stories, Ballads, and Traditions of the People*. New York: Crown Publishers, 1944.

Botkin, B. A. *A Treasury of Southern Folklore: Stories, Ballads, Traditions, and Folkways of the People of the South*. New York: Crown Publishers, 1949.

Bottigherimer, Ruth B., ed. *Fairy Tales and Society: Illusion, Allusion, and Paradigm*. Philadelphia: University of Pennsylvania Press, 1986.

Brewer, J. Mason, ed. *American Negro Folklore*. New York: Quadrangle/The New York Times Book Co., 1968.

Bruchac, Joseph. *The Iroquois Stories: Heroes and Heroines, Monsters and Magic*. Freedom, California: The Crossing Press, 1985.

Burrison, John A., ed. *Storytellers: Folktales and Legends from the South*. Athens, Georgia: University of Georgia Press, 1991.

Cameron, Anne. *Daughters of Copper Woman*. Vancouver, Canada: Press Gang Publishers, 1981.

Campbell, Joseph. *The Flight of the Wild Gander: Explorations in the Mythological Dimensions of Fairy Tales, Legends and Symbols*. New York: Harper Perennial, 1990.

Campbell, Marie. *Tales from the Cloud Walking Country*. Bloomington: Indiana University Press, 1958.

Carmer, Carl. *The Hurricane's Children: Tales from Your Neck o' the Woods*. New York: Farrar & Rinehart, Inc., 1937.

Carter, Angela. *The Bloody Chamber*. New York: Harper & Row, Publishers, Inc., 1979.

Carter, Angela, ed. *The Old Wives' Fairy Tale Book*. New York: Pantheon, 1990.

Carter, Angela, ed. *Strange Things Sometimes Still Happen: Fairy Tales from Around the World*. Boston: Faber and Faber, 1993.

Cashdan, Sheldon. *The Witch Must Die: How Fairy Tales Shape Our Lives*. New York: Basic Books/Perseus Books Group, 1999.

Chase, Richard, reteller. *Grandfather Tales: American-English Folk Tales*. Boston: Houghton Mifflin Company, 1948.

Chase, Richard. *The Jack Tales*. Boston: Houghton Mifflin Company, 1943.

Chestnutt, Charles W. *The Conjure Woman*. Originally published in 1899. New introduction by Robert M. Farnsworth. Ann Arbor: Ann Arbor Paperbacks/University of Michigan Press, 1969.

Christiansen, Reidar Th. *European Folklore in America: Studies Norvegica No. 12.* Oslo, Norway: Scandinavian University Books/Universitesforlaget, 1962.

Climo, Shirley, reteller. *A Serenade of Mermaids: Mermaid Tales from Around the World.* New York: HarperCollins Publishers, 1997.

Clough, Ben C., ed. *The American Imagination at Work: Tall Tales and Folk Tales.* New York: Alfred A. Knopf, 1947.

Coffin, Tristram Potter. *The Female Hero in Folklore and Legend.* New York: The Seabury Press, 1975; reprinted, New York: Pocket Books/Simon & Schuster, 1978.

Cohen, Anne B. *Poor Pearl! Poor Girl! The Murdered-Girl Stereotype in Ballad and Newspaper.* Austin: University of Texas Press, 1973.

Cole, Joanna, ed. *Best-Loved Folktales of the World.* New York: Doubleday, 1982.

Cornillon, Susan Koppelman, ed. *Images of Women in Fiction: Feminist Perspectives.* Bowling Green, Ohio: Bowling Green University Popular Press, 1972.

Cox, Marian Roalfe. *Cinderella.* London: David Nutt, 1893.

Curtis, Edward S., collector, and John Bierhorst, ed. *The Girl Who Married a Ghost and Other Tales from the North American Indian.* New York: Four Winds Press/Scholastic Press, 1978.

de Aragon, Ray John. *The Legend of La Llorona.* Las Vegas, New Mexico: The Pan-American Publishing Company, 1980.

de Van Etten, Theresa Pijoan. *Spanish-American Folktales: The Practical Wisdom of Spanish-Americans in 28 Eloquent and Simple Stories.* Little Rock: August House, 1990.

Drake, Samuel Adams. *A Book of New England Legends and Folklore,* 1884; revised edition published, Boston: Little, Brown, and Company, Inc., 1971, 1978.

Dundes, Alan. *Mother Wit from the Laughing Barrel: Readings in the Interpretation of Afro-American Folklore.* New York: Garland Publishing, Inc., 1981.

Dundes, Alan, ed. *Cinderella: A Casebook.* Madison: University of Wisconsin Press, 1982, 1988.

Edmonds, Margot, and Ella E. Clark. *Voices of the Winds: Native American Legends.* New York: Facts on File, Inc., 1989.

Edwards, Carolyn McVickar. *The Storyteller's Goddess: Tales of the Goddess and Her Wisdom from Around the World.* San Francisco: Harper San Francisco, 1991.

Emerson, Nathaniel B. *Pele and Hiiaka: A Myth from Hawaii;* reprint of a text originally published in 1915. Rutland, Vermont: Charles E. Tuttle Company, 1978.

Erdoes, Richard. *Tales from the American Frontier.* New York: Pantheon Books, 1991.

Erdoes, Richard, and Alfonso Ortiz. *American Indian Myths and Legends.* New York: Pantheon Books, 1984.

Estes, Clarissa Pinkola. *Women Who Run with the Wolves: Myths and Stories of the Wild Woman Archetype.* New York: Ballantine Books, 1992.

Fohr, Samuel Denis. *Cinderella's Gold Slipper: Spiritual Symbolism in the Grimms' Tales.* Wheaton, Illinois: The Theosophical Publishing House, 1991.

Gardner, Emelyn Elizabeth. *Folklore from the Scoharie Hills, New York.* Ann Arbor: University of Michigan Press, 1937.

Gernant, Karen. *Imagining Women: Fujian Folk Tales.* New York: Interlink Books, 1995.

Goodrich, Norma Lorre. *Guinevere.* New York: HarperCollins, 1991.

Goss, Linda, and Marian E. Barnes, eds. *Talk That Talk: An Anthology of African-American Storytelling.* New York: Simon & Schuster, 1989.

Haviland, Virginia, ed. *North American Legends.* New York: William Collins, 1979.

Heath, Jennifer. *On the Edge of Dream: The Women of Celtic Myth and Legend.* New York: Penguin Putnam Inc., 1998.

Hurston, Zora Neale. *Mules and Men,* originally published in 1935; reprinted, New York: HarperCollins, 1990.

Husain, Shahrukh, ed. *Daughters of the Moon: Witch Tales from Around the World.* Boston: Faber and Faber, 1994.

Jackson, Bruce, ed. *The Negro and His Folklore: In Nineteenth-Century Periodicals.* Austin: The University of Texas Press, 1977.

Jacoby, Mario, Verena Kast and Ingrid Riedel. *Witches, Ogres, and the Devil's Daughter: Encounters with Evil in Fairy Tales.* Boston: Shambhala Publications, Inc., 1992.

Jordan, Rosan A., and Susan J. Kalcik, eds. *Women's Folklore, Women's Culture (Publications of the American Folklore Society,* new series, vol. 8). Philadelphia: University of Pennsylvania Press, 1985.

Kavanagh, Linda, Sue Russell, et al. *Rapunzel's Revenge: Fairytales for Feminists.* Dublin: Attic Press, 1985.

Kerényi, Karl. *Goddesses of Sun and Moon.* Dallas, Texas: Spring Publications, Inc., 1979.

Kingston, Maxine Hong. *The Woman Warrior: Memoirs of a Girlhood Among Ghosts.* New York: Alfred A. Knopf, Inc., 1976; reprinted, New York: Vintage International, 1989.

Koltuv, Barbara Black. *The Book of Lilith.* York Beach, Maine: Nicolas-Hays, Inc., 1986.

Kraus, Anne Marie. *Folktale Themes and Activities for Children, Volume 1: Pourquoi Tales.* Englewood, Colorado: Teacher Ideas Press/A Division of Libraries Unlimited, Inc., 1999.

Kraus, Anne Marie. *Folktale Themes and Activities for Children, Volume 2: Trickster and Transformation Tales.* Englewood, Colorado: Teacher Ideas Press/A Division of Libraries Unlimited, Inc., 1999.

Larrington, Carolyne, ed. *The Feminist Companion to Mythology.* London: Pandora Press/HarperCollins Publishers, 1992.

Laurie, Alison, reteller. *Clever Gretchen and Other Forgotten Folktales.* New York: Harper & Row, 1980.

Leach, Maria, ed. *Funk and Wagnalls Standard Dictionary of Folklore, Mythology, and Legend: An Unabridged Edition of the Original Work with a Key to Place Names, Cultures, and People Discussed.* New York: Harper & Row, Publishers, Inc., 1949, 1950, 1972; paperback reprint, San Francisco: Harper San Francisco, 1984.

Lee, Tanith. *Red as Blood: Tales from the Sisters Grimmer.* New York: Daw Books, 1983.

Leeming, David, and Page, Jake. *Goddess: Myths of the Female Divine.* New York: Oxford University Press, 1994.

Lewis, Naomi, ed. *The Silent Playmate: A Collection of Doll Stories.* London: Victor Gollancz Ltd., 1979.

Lyons, Mary E. *Sorrow's Kitchen: The Life and Folklore of Zora Neale Hurston.* New York: Macmillan Publishing Company, 1990.

Malcomson, Anne Burnett. *Yankee Doodle's Cousins.* Boston: Houghton Mifflin Company, 1941.

Markale, Jean. *Women of the Celts.* Rochester, Vermont: Inner Traditions International, Ltd., 1972.

Marriott, Alice, and Carol K. Rachlin. *Plains Indians Mythology.* New York: Thomas Y. Crowell Company, 1975.

Mathias, Elizabeth, and Richard Raspa. *Italian Folktales in America: The Verbal Art of an Immigrant Woman.* Detroit: Wayne State University Press, 1985.

McCarty, Toni. *The Skull in the Snow and Other Folktales.* New York: Delacorte, 1981.

McCrickard, Janet. *Eclipse of the Sun: An Investigation into Sun and Moon Myths.* Somerset, Great Britain: Gothic Images Publications, 1990.

Minard, Rosemary, ed. *Womenfolk and Fairytales.* Boston: Houghton Mifflin Company, 1975.

Mitchell, Edwin Valentine. *Yankee Folk.* New York: The Vanguard Press, Inc., 1948.

Monaghan, Patricia. *The Book of Goddesses and Heroines.* Rev. ed., St. Paul, Minnesota: Llewellyn Publications, 1990.

Montepio, Susan N. "Women in Chinese Folktales." Article in *Folklore and Mythology Studies.*

Moon, Sheila. *Changing Woman and Her Sisters: Feminine Aspects of Selves and Deities.* San Francisco: Guild for Psychological Studies Publishing House, 1984.

Mullett, G. M. *Spider Woman Stories: Legends of the Hopi Indians.* Tucson: University of Arizona Press, 1979.

Murdock, Maureen. *The Heroine's Journey: Women's Quest for Wholeness.* Boston: Shambhala Publications, Inc., 1990.

Olson, Carl, ed. *The Book of the Goddess Past and Present: An Introduction to Her Religion.* New York: Crossroad Publishing Company, 1983.

Phelps, Ethel Johnston. *The Maid of the North: Feminist Folktales from Around the World.* New York: Holt, Rinehart and Winston, 1981.

Philip, Neil. *The Cinderella Story: The Origins and Variations of the Story Known as "Cinderella."* New York: Penguin Books, 1989.

Pogrebin, Letty, ed. *Stories for Free Children.* New York: McGraw Hill, 1982.

Putnam, Emily James. *The Lady: Studies of Certain Significant Phases of Her History.* New York: G. P. Putnam's Sons, 1910; reprinted Chicago: The University of Chicago Press, 1969.

Randolph, Vance. *The Devil's Pretty Daughter and Other Ozark Folktales, with Notes by Herbert Halpert.* New York: Columbia University Press, 1955.

Randolph, Vance. *Sticks in the Knapsack and Other Ozark Folk Tales.* New York: Columbia University Press, 1958.

Randolph, Vance. *The Talking Turtle and Other Ozark Folk Tales.* New York: Columbia University Press, 1957.

Randolph, Vance. *Who Blowed Up the Church House? and Other Ozark Folk Tales*. New York: Columbia University Press, 1952.

Reiter, Joan Swallow. *The Women (The Old West,* vol. 23). Alexandria, Virginia: Time-Life Books, 1978.

Reynard, Elizabeth. *The Narrow Land: Folk Chronicles of Old Cape Cod*. Boston and New York: Houghton Mifflin Company, 1934.

Riordan, James. *The Woman in the Moon and Other Tales of Forgotten Heroines*. New York: Dial Books for Young Readers, 1985.

Roberts, Leonard W. *Old Greasybeard: Tales from the Cumberland Gap*. Detroit: Folklore Associates, 1969.

Roberts, Leonard W. *Say Branch Settlers: Folksongs and Tales of a Kentucky Mountain Family*. Austin: The University of Texas Press, 1974.

Roberts, Leonard W. *South from Hell-fer-Sartin: Kentucky Mountain Folk Tales*. Lexington: University of Kentucky Press, 1955; reprinted 1988.

Roberts, Leonard W. *Up Cutshin and Down Greasy*. Lexington: University of Kentucky Press, 1959.

Salmonson, Jessica Amanda. *The Encyclopedia of Amazons: Women Warriors from Antiquity to the Modern Era*. New York: Paragon House, 1991.

Seagraves, Anne. *Women of the Sierra*. Lakeport, California: Wesanne Enterprises, 1990.

Shay, Frank. *Here's Audacity! American Legendary Heroes*. Freeport, New York: Books for Libraries, Inc., 1967 reprint of book originally copyright in 1930.

Silko, Leslie Marmon. *Storyteller*. New York: Seaver Books, 1981.

Simmons, William S. *Spirit of the New England Tribes: Indian History and Folklore, 1620–1984*. Hanover and London: University Press of New England, 1986.

Stone, Kay. "Things Walt Disney Never Told Us." Essay in the "Women and Folklore" issue of the New York: *Journal of American Folklore,* vol. 88 (January-March 1975).

Strachey, Marjorie. *Savitri and Other Women*. New York: G. P. Putnam's Sons, 1921.

Trinh, T. Minh-Ha. *Woman Native Other: Writing Postcoloniality and Feminism*. Bloomington: Indiana University Press, 1989.

Vigil, Angel, reteller. *The Corn Woman: Stories and Legends of the Hispanic Southwest*. Englewood, Colorado: Libraries Unlimited Inc., 1994.

Voth, Anne. *Women in the New Eden: The Stories of Six American Women*. Washington, D.C.: University Press of America, 1983.

Williams, Jay. *The Practical Princess and Other Liberating Tales*. New York: Scholastic, Inc., 1973.

Yolen, Jane, ed. *Favorite Folktales from Around the World*. New York: Pantheon Books, 1986.

Zipes, Jack. *Don't Bet on the Prince: Contemporary Feminist Fairy Tales in North America and England*. New York: Methuen, Inc., 1986.

Zipes, Jack, ed. *The Outspoken Princess and the Gentle Knight: A Treasury of Modern Fairy Tales*. New York: Bantam Books, 1994.

**Robert D. San Souci** is the author of *The Talking Eggs*, a 1990 Caldecott Honor Book and Coretta Scott King Honor Book, *The Samurai's Daughter*, *The Hired Hand*, and many other award-winning books, most of which are based on legend, myth, folklore, and history. He lives in San Francisco, California.

**Brian Pinkney** has illustrated many award-winning children's books, including Robert D. San Souci's *The Faithful Friend*, a 1996 Caldecott Honor Book and Coretta Scott King Honor Book. Mr. Pinkney received a 1999 Caldecott Honor for *Duke Ellington: The Piano Prince and His Orchestra*, by his wife Andrea Davis Pinkney, and also illustrated her book, *Seven Candles for Kwanzaa*. The Pinkneys live in Brooklyn, New York.